Purchased from c

FLASHPOINT

by
D.A. Richardson

TRAFFORD
Canada · UK · Ireland · USA

© Copyright 2004 Debra Anne Richardson. All rights reserved.

No part of this publication may be reproduced, stored in a retrieval system, or transmitted, in any form or by any means, electronic, mechanical, photocopying, recording, or otherwise, without the written prior permission of the author.

Cover art by John Brown.

Printed in Victoria, Canada

Note for Librarians: a cataloguing record for this book that includes Dewey Classification and US Library of Congress numbers is available from the National Library of Canada. The complete cataloguing record can be obtained from the National Library's online database at: www.nlc-bnc.ca/amicus/index-e.html

ISBN 1-4120-1671-1

TRAFFORD

This book was published *on-demand* **in cooperation with Trafford Publishing.** On-demand publishing is a unique process and service of making a book available for retail sale to the public taking advantage of on-demand manufacturing and Internet marketing. **On-demand publishing** includes promotions, retail sales, manufacturing, order fulfilment, accounting and collecting royalties on behalf of the author.

Suite 6E, 2333 Government St., Victoria, B.C. V8T 4P4, CANADA
Phone   250-383-6864   Toll-free   1-888-232-4444 (Canada & US)
Fax   250-383-6804   E-mail   sales@trafford.com
Web site   www.trafford.com   TRAFFORD PUBLISHING IS A DIVISION OF TRAFFORD HOLDINGS LTD.
Trafford Catalogue #03-2048   www.trafford.com/robots/03-2048.html

10   9   8

Flashpoint

In her career as an arsonist, she had destroyed two restaurants, a bookstore and a church. She'd torched a new home construction site, the service garage of a trucking company and an apartment building. In Atlanta, she burned a racing stable and a hotel.

From city to city, she torched buildings and took the lives of firefighters – keeping the promise she made to herself at her Uncle Henry's fire department funeral.

Welcome to the world of firefighting. The smoke, sweat and tears of a job not meant for the weak of body, mind or soul. Three women will cross the paths of the crew of Fire Hall No.5, but only one will plan their death.

D.A. Richardson

This book is a work of fiction. Names, characters, places and events are a product of the Author's imagination and used purely fictitiously.

Resemblances to locations, people or events either living or dead are purely coincidental.

Dedication

Fire is a living, breathing demon with a mind all its own. It is capable of destroying everything in its path with little or no warning and can change directions with no more than a shift in the wind.

A dangerous intruder, fire can suck the life out of its victims in a matter of minutes and injures or claims the life of at least one North American firefighter every day.

Ordinary citizens call upon firefighters in their most desperate time of need. *Flashpoint* is dedicated to those firefighters; the brave men and women who risk their lives for a living, and the family support system that stands behind them.

From the Author

While doing research at the Ontario Fire College in Gravenhurst, Ontario I came across a poem that I would like to share with you. It's called the Firefighters Prayer.

When I am called to duty God
Whenever flames may rage
Give me strength to save some life
Whatever be its age

Help me embrace a little child
Before it is too late
Or save an older person
From the horror of that fate

Enable me to be alert
And hear the weakest shout
And quickly and efficiently
To put the fire out

I want to fill my calling
And give the best in me
To guard my every neighbor
And protect his property

And if according to my fate
I am to lose my life
Please bless with your protective hand
My children and my wife

(Author unknown)

Acknowledgement

I thank the City of Calgary, Fire Department Headquarters, for allowing me the opportunity to experience the job of firefighting first hand. The management, office, and training staff of the Calgary Fire Department Training Academy, for letting me hang out with them. It was quite a rush!

The training officers put me through the paces and taught me what firefighting is all about. The recruits from Class I – 2000 and Class III – 2001 gave it all a personal touch.

I thank the Calgary Fire Prevention Bureau, the Kalispell Fire Department, the management, office and training staff of the Ontario Fire College, and the hundreds of firefighters I spoke with from one end of the country to the other.

A very special thanks to the Captains and Crews of No. 9 for welcoming me into their hall to share their laughter, their sorrow and many a good meal. Without their input, *Flashpoint* would not have come to life.

Flash point: *n* : the lowest temperature at which vapors above a volatile combustible substance ignite in air when exposed to flame.
(Webster's Dictionary)

PART ONE

Chapter One

Denver – 2000

IT HAD BEEN EASY getting information on setting fires. She started at the public library when she was fifteen. Over the years, she'd read everything she could get her hands on. She learned about 'V' patterns; a term used to describe a particular burn pattern left in the aftermath of a fire. Its unique 'V' shape, was caused by the flames traveling upward, and outward, from their point of origin.

She learned that a 'fire trail' was the evidence left behind from a fuse made of a liquid accelerant such as gasoline, or a vapor accelerant like rolled up paper. Fire trails could be a major clue in an arson investigation and she created a great one when she set fire to her uncle's fishing lodge seventeen years ago.

While Uncle Henry was in the main dining room entertaining his guests, she took his apartment key from behind the registration desk and snuck into his room. She squeezed a blob of airplane glue on the carpet at the side of the bed, just behind the bed skirt, and ran a trail of glue across the carpet in the bedroom, down the hall, and across the linoleum kitchen floor to the window.

She knew Henry would be half pissed when he got back to his room. She also knew that he smoked in bed. The last thing he did before he went to sleep at night was have a cigarette. Tonight, it would cost him his life – or at least the fire department would think so.

When she was sure he'd passed out, she climbed up the white trellis at the side of the lodge and crawled across the roof to the kitchen window of the apartment. She quietly pushed up the window, leaned in and reached down until she felt the glob of glue she'd left earlier. When she lit it, her fire trail burned its way into Henry's room. There, it set fire to the bed with him in it.

***

Her first fire had been a challenge but each one got easier. In fact, she was becoming quite a pro at it. In the past eight months alone she'd set three fires, all of which had completely gutted the buildings and caused hundreds of thousands of dollars in damage.

In her career as an arsonist, she destroyed two restaurants, a bookstore and a church. She'd torched a new home construction site, the service garage of a trucking company and an apartment building. In Atlanta, she burned a racing stable and a hotel.

It gave her a great feeling of satisfaction when she'd read in the paper that the fires were arson-related but there were no suspects. She'd never be a suspect; she didn't fit the profile. She could bump off firefighters from one end of the country to the other and they'd never catch her.

According to her research, the typical arsonist was a loner. She loved to socialize. The typical arsonist had a motive for setting the fire: Sometimes it was an insurance scam, other times to cover up a crime. She wasn't a pyromaniac: she didn't get sexual satisfaction from setting her fires, she got sexual revenge.

Rarely, did she try to hide the fire's point of origin. More often than not, she left fire trails from one end of the building to the other. She didn't care if arson investigators knew the fires were deliberately set.

Her choice of accelerants ranged from gasoline and paint thinner to vegetable oil and alcohol. She used her man-made flames to entice firefighters into the building. Once inside, they fell victim to her traps.

She'd learned some new tricks over the years and with each one, she took the life of another firefighter. In St. Louis, she bagged two of them. One was a guy she'd been dating for a month. He may have been a lousy lay, but he was a wealth of knowledge. His little story gave her some great ideas.

"It was twenty years ago, when I was just a rookie," he began. "We got the call about 10:30 pm. Someone phoned 911 and reported seeing smoke coming from St. Peter's. They'd been right. When we arrived on scene, there was smoke showing from the top of the church.

"While we were masking up, the caretaker told us that they'd been doing renovations inside. They were putting in a new air conditioning system. He thought, maybe, one of the construction guys left something on somewhere. So, we went in to investigate.

"There was no smoke in the main part of the chapel, so my partner figured we should run a ladder up the scuttle hole and have a look around the attic. We didn't have a hose line with us, all we were gonna do, was see if we could find the seat of the fire. The incoming rigs would make the hydrant.

"Back in those days, we didn't carry radios like we do today. When we found the fire, we had to relay the information to the rest of the crew in person. We didn't carry personal alarm systems in case we went down, and we didn't have flash hoods as part of our gear. We didn't have a lot of things back then.

"Anyway, we climbed up through the hole to take a look in the attic. Look, that was a joke! With the heavy smoke and the obstruction of my mask, I couldn't see more than two feet in front of me. I was scared shitless.

"We started wandering around looking for the fire. The further we walked towards the back of the church, the thicker the smoke got. I was having a real hard time seeing my partner.

"We'd gone no more than about twenty feet when all of a sudden the floor was gone and I felt my stomach in my throat. I dropped about four feet and came to a grinding halt. My mind started racing trying to figure out what happened. My senior man had been in front of me, now he was gone. I actually thought it might be his body that broke my fall.

"I fought like a tiger trying to free myself, but it was impossible. I was trapped. My left leg and left arm were pinned at my side. My right arm was above my head, my right leg behind me. I was in, whatever I was in, up to my chest.

"When I finally made sense of everything, I figured out that I'd fallen into an open air conditioning shaft but I had no idea where my partner had gone.

"I must admit, I had a moment of panic when I realized I was alone. It was getting hotter than hell and my ears were starting to burn. I looked for something to grab on to and pull myself up, but it was useless. Even if I'd found something, all I could do was wave my right arm above my head.

"When I stared ahead into the blackness, I saw a faint orange glow and I knew I'd found the seat of the fire. As the glow got brighter, the smoke seemed to be getting lighter. Before long, I realized that the fire was coming right at me. I remember chuckling to myself thinking this was the first time I'd been in a church in a long time and it was probably gonna be my last.

"Then, the weirdest thing happened. A real feeling of tranquility swept over me and I calmed right down. My heart stopped pounding. My pulse stopped racing and I started breathing normal again. It was the strangest sensation I'd ever had. I knew I was ready to die.

"I also knew that it would only be a matter of minutes. The fire was no more than fifteen feet away from me and I could see it starting to curl over my head. I took a deep breath, closed my eyes and waited for death. Then, out of nowhere, someone grabbed me from behind and popped me out of the hole like a cork out of a champagne bottle."

***

The information she gathered that night helped her kill a firefighter in Phoenix. When he tried to save the new home construction site she set fire to, he fell through the holes she'd cut in the floor.

In Detroit, a firefighter perished when she set fire to the

service garage of Jake's Trucking Company. Thanks to the owner's son, without him even realizing it, he'd helped her set the trap.

She told him she was looking for used tires for her boss. She liked the ones on the top shelf. He pulled them part way off the storage rack and propped them up with two twelve foot, two by fours. He'd leave the tires that way until her boss had a chance to come by and look at them the next day.

Before she started the fire that night, she wrapped the base of each wooden pole with gasoline soaked rags. When the poles burned, the tires would crash to the ground crushing anyone who happened to be standing under them.

At the opposite end of the garage, she poured a jerry can of gasoline over the tires on the display rack. The burning rubber would create a cloud of smoke the color of coal, making it impossible for firefighters to see the trap they were walking into.

It had been a hot, black, dirty fire and she watched the whole thing on the news channel from the comfort of her own living room.

Tonight, she would take care of firefighter Brad Walker, the same way she'd taken care of Travis Greenwood in Chicago.

Chapter Two

Chicago – one year earlier

IT WAS 22:00 WHEN she climbed the front steps of Chicago Fire Department Headquarters. She'd come with one thing in mind: come hell or high water, she had to get into the file room. She needed some new ideas and she couldn't think of a better place to get them.

Her father's estate was drying up, thanks to that bitch he'd married. But, after bedding the owner of the insurance company he'd dealt with, she discovered that the fire insurance policy on his racing stable would get her close to half a million. Even more, if the best horses happened to be inside.

When she opened the front door of fire headquarters, twenty-four year old rookie firefighter Travis Greenwood was manning his post at the front desk.

"Piece of cake," she whispered under her breath as she ran her hands down the curves of her streamlined body to straighten her silk blouse and black leather skirt. *Men are such fools. All it takes is a smile, a little skin, and they give you whatever you want.*

She'd learned over the years that her body was her greatest asset and she used it to her full advantage. It was tall and lean, and attracted men like flies to honey. Now, it would help her cut through the red tape and allow her to get the information she'd come in search of.

She took a deep breath, put on a seductive grin, and walked towards Travis with the style of a Paris runway model. "Oh, Travis. I'm so glad you're here," she began in her sweet southern drawl. "I feel so foolish, and I desperately need your help."

A goofy boyish grin lit up his face. "Why, I'd do anything for you. What do you need?" He asked.

"Mrs. Stewart is back from her holidays tomorrow and I completely forgot to update one of the arson files she asked me to look after." She tipped her head slightly and offered him her best smile. "I was hoping you could let me into the investigation file room?"

Travis raised a blonde eyebrow and shook his head. "Well, I can do almost anything, except that." He flashed her a puzzled look. "I thought Karen took care of Mrs. Stewart's files?"

"Oh, she does, but she's off sick." She batted her baby blues at him. "Karen called me at home and asked me if I'd take care of this for her. That's why I'm here."

Travis scratched his clean shaved chin. "Gee, I don't know. If I let you in the file room without proper authorization, I could lose my job."

"Well," she blushed, "I guess you could say I have authorization. I've been taking care of the arson files while Karen's been off sick."

"Didn't I see her here yesterday?" Travis inquired.

You're not as stupid as you look, she told herself as she smiled back at him. Her sweet southern drawl broke the silence. "Karen was here. She came in to pick up her pay stub."

Travis let out a disappointed sigh. "You know, I'd really like to help you out, but I don't think I can."

"Oh, please Travis," she begged.

"I don't know. The rules say that no one goes into the investigation room without the proper authorization, and you know how strict they are around here about the rules."

Without taking her ice blue eyes from his, she undid the top two buttons of her silk blouse and slowly began fanning herself with her hands. "My goodness, don't you find it warm in here?" She asked in a low seductive voice.

"N-n-no," Travis stammered.

She leaned over the desk, offering the red-faced young man a better view of her cleavage. "Well," she sighed, "it's a pitiful shame that you can't help me." She stuck out her cherry-red painted lower lip in a pout. "I hope Karen doesn't lose her job because of this."

Her voice dripped with honey and Travis felt a fire building in his loins as he stared down her blouse. He blushed, imagining what it would feel like to cup her firm, round breasts in his hands. He wondered if her lips tasted as sweet as the sound that came out of them each time she spoke.

She was gorgeous, and he estimated her to be in her late twenties. She had an hourglass figure, and the longest legs he'd ever seen. Her long, dark hair and alabaster complexion only made her blue eyes all the more intriguing.

Travis had wanted to ask her out for months, but she always seemed so aloof. He'd heard that anyone brave enough to approach her had been cut off at the knees. Word amongst the guys at fire headquarters was that she was a cold fish. In fact, they'd even gone so far as to give her a nickname: they called her the 'Ice Princess.'

She seemed different tonight: the way she was dressed, the way she was acting. There was a gleam in her eyes and Travis was sure that she was trying to seduce him. *I'll show the guys around here how to melt the 'Ice Princess'.*

As she straightened up, he reached out and gently touched her arm. "No – wait." His eyes reluctantly moved upwards from her cleavage. "If you promise that you'll only be a few minutes, I guess it'll be okay."

He hoped he wasn't making a mistake. He knew that if he got caught, he'd have one hell of a black mark on his record, but it was late, and all the guys were either upstairs in the TV room, or in bed asleep. As long as she was quick, no one would be any wiser. Besides, this would be a great way to get into her good graces.

Travis took a deep breath, and reached into the top drawer for the key. "How long did you say you'd be?"

"Five minutes, tops," she smiled.

He nervously bit the corner of his lip. "Okay, but no longer."

"No longer, I promise." She grabbed his bright, red face in

her hands and gave him a huge smack on the lips. "Oh Travis, you're a life saver. I owe you one."

"Great," he replied with a beaming grin. "How about coming over to my place for a drink sometime?"

"Why, Mr. Greenwood," she blushed. "I thought you would never ask."

In the investigation file room, she found a copy of the Confidential Accelerants list. It told her which accelerants were virtually undetectable. She also found valuable information on different types of incinerating devices and fuses. She read through several of the current arson investigations and gathered little tidbits that she could use the next time she decided to light up the night sky.

One file in particular suggested a better method of using gasoline. Instead of just throwing it around the room and leaving a fire trail, she could spray it, or paint it on the walls, making its presence virtually undetectable to arson investigators.

Chapter Three

HER PLAN THAT NIGHT had been brilliant, but she'd discovered over the years that her most valuable information had come from firefighters themselves. It was amazing what some of them would tell you when they'd had a few too many cocktails.

A satisfied smile swept across her face as she pulled Travis's apartment key from her coat pocket. She hadn't planned on setting this fire, but perhaps it was appropriate to leave the 'Windy City' in a blaze of glory!

Last week, she'd attended her farewell luncheon. She'd laid the groundwork for her departure weeks earlier by telling co-workers that her father was ailing and she was moving to Atlanta to be with him.

After opening her gift of a beautiful fourteen carat gold Chicago Fire Department ring, she smiled the smile that could melt an iceberg and gave Mrs. Stewart a warm hug. "Why, it just breaks my heart to have to leave all of you and this beautiful city."

"Take care of yourself," they all told her. "And, keep in touch."

They all liked her. What wasn't to like? She was pleasant, charming, and a very proficient worker. And, best of all, no one had ever suspected that a shy timid southern belle was capable of such deadly destruction.

She knew she would miss Chicago, particularly the wail of sirens that told her something, somewhere, was on fire, but she promised herself that once she was settled in a new city, she would hear the sirens again.

The demented laugh that erupted from her chest as she closed the apartment door behind her would have sent a cold chill up the spine of anyone who was listening, but she knew that the occupant of the eleventh floor, corner suite apartment wouldn't hear her. Thanks to her little concoction, Travis Greenwood was passed out cold. Earlier, she'd slipped him a Mickey Finn and she knew that he wouldn't be waking up anytime soon. In fact, she knew that he'd never wake up again.

The thought made her smile as she walked down the hallway to his bedroom. "God, I'm good," she proclaimed as she stared down at Travis's lifeless body. He hadn't moved since she'd helped him get to his king size bed two hours earlier. "Don't go away," she laughed. "I'll be right back."

She pulled a screwdriver from her pocket and began making her way through the apartment replacing the charged batteries in the smoke detectors with dead ones. Next, she went into the living room and tipped over the half empty bottle of Jack Daniel's that sat on the coffee table. Her eyes twinkled with delight as she watched the amber liquid soak into the carpet.

In the kitchen, she dug through an ashtray of cigarette butts until she found one that was appropriate. "This will do." She pulled it from the pile and wiped the ashes off on her jeans. She stuck the half-smoked butt between her lips and turned on the stove. When the burner was red hot, she bent down to greet it, sucking and puffing on the stale filter until smoke rose in the air above her head.

On her way back to the living room, she took a long, satisfying drag and blew smoke circles as she exhaled. It was a trick she'd learned from Uncle Henry when she was eleven.

"It's easy, kiddo," he would say, taking her face in his hands and maneuvering her mouth until she looked as if she were about to sing the American National Anthem. "Now, just blow."

She turned the whiskey bottle upright and placed the ashtray she was carrying on the table beside it. She took one more drag and this time, blew at the end of the cigarette until the cherry burned red-hot. She dropped the butt on the table and watched as it ate away at the wood beneath it. When it had burned down to the filter and she was sure it was out, she picked it up and laid it on the alcohol soaked carpet. Arson investigators would think the cigarette had fallen from the ashtray.

She knew that after the fire, police and fire arson investigators would comb the area talking to witnesses. They would talk to the officer who was in command of the fire. They would talk to the firefighters who were first on scene and ask them if they'd noticed anything strange, or if they had problems getting to the fire. The answers to the questions would be added to the pieces of the puzzle collected inside Travis's apartment.

Next, she was sure that Bart Campbell, Chicago's lead fire arson investigator, would take charge. He was a bulldog and he'd stop at nothing until he found the cause of the blaze. He would take pictures of the lobby and the stairwell in Travis's building. On the eleventh floor, Bart would photograph the hallway leading up to Travis's apartment. Inside the apartment, as he did with every fire investigation, he would take pictures of every square inch of every room.

He would start in the kitchen and work his way through the living room, dining room and down the hallway to the bedroom. He would look for clues leading him to the most severe burn damage, and hunt for 'V' patterns, and fire trails to determine where the fire started. When Bart began removing and examining the debris left in the aftermath of her little bonfire, he would find Travis's body in the rubble.

As she walked back to the bedroom, the sound of batteries jingling in her pocket was music to her ears. She knew that Travis wouldn't cough from the smoke as it started to fill his room. The smoke detectors wouldn't go off, to wake him from his drug induced stupor. He wouldn't feel the heat of the flames eating away at his flesh until it was too late. Her blue eyes sparkled as she visualized his demise.

From ten to fourteen minutes, Travis's arms and legs would become badly charred. At fifteen to twenty minutes, the bones would begin to become visible on his face and arms, then his ribs and skull. By thirty-five minutes, the bones of his upper and lower legs would be exposed.

As Travis's body gave into the extreme heat, the muscles of his arms and legs would constrict. His tongue would protrude from his mouth, and the muscles of his face and neck would contract. His skin would split apart, and the build-up of steam from his internal fluids would cause the vault of his abdomen to rupture.

The last step in his cremation would come due to a lack of moisture. His body would go into progressive desiccation and dry out until it carbonized and the crystals of his bones fused together.

A satisfied smile swept across her face. "With any luck, there won't be enough left of you to warrant an autopsy, Mr. Greenwood."

She was sure the coroner would conclude that the fire had killed Travis, but she knew better. By the time arson investigators realized that the fire had been deliberately set, she would be long gone.

"Travis, my dear, sweet Travis." She bent down and sensually brushed her lips against his ear. "If you would have just kept your hands to yourself," she whispered, "this wouldn't have had to happen. I wouldn't have to punish you like this."

She straightened the collar of his blue polo shirt and ran her long graceful fingers through his thick, strawberry blonde hair. As she stood up, she let out a long daunting sigh. "If you would have just shared your information with me and left it at that, but no," she frowned, "you figured you deserved something in return." Their earlier conversation flashed through her mind.

"Oh, it's easy to set a fire sweetheart. In fact, you can start an electrical fire and be out the door long before the first hint of smoke," Travis had told her in his drug induced stupor. "All you do is take the cover off an electrical outlet, stuff a cube of barbecue starter inside, light it, put the cover back on, and walk away. Thomas Edison will take care of the rest."

Travis had provided the information only moments before

reaching across the table, grabbing her left breast and asking, "so baby, you want to slide down my fire pole?"

He had mauled her when she'd asked him not to. As far as she was concerned, men were all the same. They drank too much and shot their mouths off. They slobbered and drooled, and touched you in places you didn't want to be touched. They made you do things you didn't want to do.

She shook off the sickening reminder of her youth and checked her watch. *Perfect, I can get all of my shopping done and be back at the hotel in time for afternoon cocktails.*

She knew from years of studying fire what made it burn and what snuffed it out. Oxygen was the key ingredient. Before she left, she would close Travis's bedroom door to cut off the air supply from the rest of the apartment. The fire would burn inside the room until it had sucked every last breath of oxygen from the air. Then, it would lie dormant, sometimes for hours, until oxygen was re-introduced into the equation. The minute Travis's roommate opened the bedroom door all hell would break loose. Oxygen would rush into the room and there would be an explosion, a backdraft that would cause the entire suite to go up in a blaze of glory.

She checked her watch again. "If I timed it right," she smiled, "911 should be getting the call right about shift change." She knew if the call came in around 5:30 pm when the day shift was leaving and the night shift was arriving, it would slow down the fire hall's response time. Something else in her favor would be the rush hour traffic. Downtown streets would be in gridlock.

She pushed the button on the side of her watch and set the timer for 5:45 pm. She walked to the bed, touched her index finger to her lips, and then to Travis's. "Goodnight, sweet prince. Thanks for the memories."

When she turned around, she caught a glimpse of Travis's fire department ring resting on the night table. She picked it up and examined it. The blue sapphire stone was set in gold. Engraved on one side was the Chicago Fire Department crest. On the other, the year 1999. She rolled the ring over and over in her fingers before dropping it into her coat pocket. "Perfect, something old, something new and now something blue. All I need is something borrowed and a husband!"

She reached into her jeans, pulled out a small square of tinfoil, and nonchalantly unfolded the corners. She knew that in order to support free burning, the fire triangle required three elements: oxygen, fuel and heat. Without one of them, there could be no fire. A stimulating rush raced up her spine, and her body tingled with delight as she lodged the white cube of barbecue starter into the electrical outlet beside Travis's bed. The barbecue starter would provide the initial spark, but she was sure that when Bart Campbell showed up tomorrow and saw the 'V' pattern above the socket, he would think the fire had been caused by a short circuit in the electrical system.

With a satisfied grin on her face, she lit the match. She replaced the cover, stood up, and backed away, confident that a small flame was now making its way up the wires behind the drywall. Soon, sparks would shoot from the socket and extend their fingers outwards until they made contact with the drapes. From there, the flames would spread upward, eating away at the material. The drapes would burn off the rod, drop to the floor, and set the carpet between the window and the bed on fire. Within minutes, Travis's body would be surrounded by an orange glow.

Once the fire had sucked the oxygen from the air, it would snuff itself out. There would be no more flames, but the deadly gases from unburned material would continue to build and grow until they had filled the bedroom. The gases would ooze their way under the closed bedroom door and through the ventilation system, swirling and dancing down the hallway to the den, the living room, dining room and kitchen. When they had occupied every available space, they would hang in the air, becoming more explosive by the minute.

As she walked towards the front door, she caught the faint whiff of smoke and she knew the wheels had been set in motion. The aroma wasn't that of a pleasant wood burning fire, but the odor of plastic, paint and deadly fumes. "Burn in hell," she remarked as she backed into the hallway and closed the apartment door.

"Hello, dear."

The voice startled her and a gasp escaped from her throat. She quickly spun around and offered the five-foot-five, portly, gray haired woman an anxious smile. "Hello," her voice trembled.

"Is Travis home?" The old woman asked.

The brunette took a breath to compose herself. "Yes. He is," she answered back, "but he's just laid down. I'm afraid he's not feeling well. A little too much partying last night." She gave the woman a reassuring smile. "I'm sure he'll be fine once he sleeps it off."

"Well, he better be fine, we have a dinner engagement tonight." The old woman shook her head and gave the attractive brunette a puzzled look. "Wait a minute. Travis couldn't have been partying last night. He was at work last night. He's a fireman you know." She stuck out her hand. "My name is Betty Hobson. Are you a friend of ..."

"Betty, I don't mean to be rude," the brunette interrupted, "but I really must go. I'm late for an appointment."

She turned on her heels and quickly headed towards the elevator, thankful that Travis's apartment was practically airtight. Betty Hobson, or anyone else for that matter, wouldn't be able to smell the smoke even if they stood at his front door. It would be hours before anyone realized that something was burning inside apartment 1110.

After leaving Travis's apartment, she went shopping and purchased a ten thousand-dollar fur coat. She put it on her American Express card knowing that by the time the bill caught up to her, she'd have the insurance money from burning down her father's racing stable. At the jeweler's, a beautiful diamond pendant caught her eye. Her last stop before checking into her suite at Le Meridean Hotel on North Michigan Avenue, was a trip to the hair salon. The new style and color were very becoming, but she knew she would miss her long dark mane.

By 4:00 pm she was settled in her hotel room. She had a

long hot Jacuzzi, and ordered a clubhouse sandwich from room service. When the timer on her watch went off, she turned on her police scanner and listened for the dispatch that she knew would come. It arrived at 6:01.

"Engine Company No. 23, Ladder Company 23, please respond to a reported apartment fire at..."

A satisfied smile swept across her face. "It's begun."

She picked up the telephone and called room service. "Hello, this is suite 1901. Would you please send up a bottle of Nipozzano Chianti and an eight-ounce filet, rare. I'll have a baked potato with butter, sour cream, bacon bits and chives. Whatever vegetable you have today will be fine. I'd like raspberry vinaigrette on the salad please, and I'll have crème caramel for dessert. I'm just about to climb into the tub, so would you please have the bellman leave the dinner cart in the living room."

A devious smile danced across her face as she hung up the phone. She raced into the dressing room of her suite where she pulled a black tracksuit and a gray fisherman knit sweater from her suitcase. In the bathroom, she dug around in her make-up bag until she found the bottle of spirit gum and the tiny box that held her fake moustache and sideburns. She checked her watch. *Room service will be here in fifteen minutes. I've got just enough time to apply my disguise and get out before dinner arrives.*

She twisted the cap off the spirit gum and applied the sticky glue to her upper lip, then to the soft skin on the sides of her face. She knew they would be taking pictures of the crowd at the scene, and she couldn't afford to be recognized.

After applying her disguise, she took a pair of black horn-rimmed glasses from her purse and slipped them on. She climbed into her tracksuit and pulled the heavy wool sweater over her head. She stood for a moment and looked at herself in the mirror. "Perfect. Not even your own grandmother would recognize you." She turned on the taps, and splashed water on her hair. Before leaving the bathroom, she hit the button for the jetted tub.

In the living room, she checked her police scanner again to get an update on the fire.

"Dispatch, this is Engine 23. We have a working fire. This is an eighteen floor, one hundred and eighty-suite, residential building. We have flames showing on the northwest corner of the eleventh floor. Engine 23 is in command at the front of the building. I'm requesting a second alarm."

She turned off the radio and tucked it under the sofa cushion. *I can't forget to pack that*, she reminded herself as she headed to the front door. She knew in order to get anywhere near the fire tonight, she'd have to be a firefighter, a police officer, or a member of the press. Lucky for her, she always carried a press pass in her pocket. She put on her Nikes, a black leather jacket, and crowned her head with a black baseball cap. With one final look in the mirror, she was out the door.

Chapter Four

SHE WAS DISAPPOINTED THAT the picture in this morning's paper hadn't done the fire justice. It was a magnificent blaze. Her best to date. The sound of knocking drew her attention away from the photo on the front page. She tossed the paper on the table and went to the door.

"Good morning, Miss," the bellboy smiled. "Did you have a pleasant evening?"

"Yes. I did," she replied, her southern drawl now absent. "In fact, it couldn't have been better." The mere thought of one less firefighter in the country brought a radiant smile to her face.

"Your limo is here to take you to the airport Miss. May I take your luggage and escort you downstairs?"

"You can take the luggage, but tell the driver I'll be a few minutes. I have to make a phone call." She gave the young man a wink, and slipped him a crisp fifty-dollar bill. "Here, take your girlfriend out for dinner."

"Thank you very much!" he exclaimed in grateful surprise. "I'll tell the driver."

She closed the door behind her and walked to the Queen Anne desk that sat in the corner of the room. She picked up the telephone and began to dial. There was no need to check the directory for the number, she knew it off by heart.

"Good morning. Chicago Fire Department," a shaky voice answered.

"Hi, Gloria. It's just me. I wanted to call and say goodbye."

"Oh, hi." The southern drawl was familiar to the Fire Chief's secretary and she knew instantly who it was. "Listen, kid," Gloria began, "can you call me when you get settled? I can't talk right now. All hell is breaking loose around here. I have to go."

"Gloria, what's wrong?"

"There was a big fire in Travis Greenwood's apartment last night," Gloria quickly replied.

"Oh, my God. Is Travis okay?" The southern drawl was filled with concern.

There was a long silent pause. "No, he isn't, he's dead. One of his neighbors was injured, and a rookie from No. 23 is in the hospital with severe burns." Gloria took a deep breath to control the quiver in her voice. "I really have to go now, the Chief needs me." With that the phone went dead.

Satisfaction danced across her face as she placed the receiver back in the cradle. "Perfect," she smiled, "two birds with one stone!"

Chapter Five

Seattle – Present Day

KURT ROPER OPENED THE front hall closet and pulled out a jerry can of gasoline. He unscrewed the cap, took out the spout, and fastened it into place. This would be a nice fire trail, one that fire arson investigators would easily spot.

He'd miss his one bedroom, ground floor, corner suite apartment but burning it was all part of his master plan to get even with Jane. He'd only managed to get her to his place once, but during her visit he introduced her to several of his neighbors. He had to make sure, that when the time came, they'd be able to identify her.

Kurt smiled as he walked down the hall to the bedroom pouring gasoline as he went. After the fire, when arson investigators lifted the burned carpet, they would discover scorch marks on the cement floor that ran from one end of the apartment to the other. Their first instinct would tell them that the fire had been deliberately set. When they tested the carpet for accelerants, they'd have their proof.

When Kurt reached the bedroom, he had just enough gasoline to make a trail from the doorway to the bed. He set the can on the floor and opened the drawer of the night table. He took out a box of wooden matches, an elastic band, and a package of Winston cigarettes.

One by one, he placed the items in a nice neat line on the night table. He turned the cigarette package on its side and flicked the bottom of it with his short chubby fingers until three filters popped from the opening. His hands shook as he fumbled to pick them up. "I need a drink." *Not yet,* he told himself. *Soon, when this is over.*

Kurt took a deep breath to calm himself and rolled the cigarettes into the shape of a triangle. He fastened them with the elastic band and set them beside the ashtray. Next, he picked up the wooden box, opened it, and took out two matches. Before he left the room, he'd light the cigarettes with his lighter and shoved the matches down between the center, wooden end first, until the red sulfur head was resting just below the filters.

Kurt placed his man-made fuse in the ashtray with one cigarette resting in the groove, the other resting above it. He'd been experimenting over the past week and discovered it took three minutes before the burning tobacco would ignite the matches. When that happened, the contraption would flip out of the ashtray, land on the carpet, ignite the gasoline trail and POOF!

Kurt knew that he'd be the first person the fire department questioned, but he'd have an airtight alibi. The arson division could look till they were blue in the face and they'd never find a reason for him to torch his own apartment. Jane, on the other hand, would be a different story. He himself had provided her with a motive.

He opened the bedroom closet door, knelt down on the floor, and ran his shaky hand over the cold gray metal of the safe. After the fire, when the firefighters were inside doing salvage and overhaul, they'd find the little steel box. What police and fire arson investigators found inside would make Jane Phillips their number one suspect in tonight's blaze.

Kurt spun the dial left, right, then left again. When the tumblers clicked, he pulled the door open and stared down at the envelope containing the information he knew would ruin Jane's career. "Now, it's time for a drink."

He pulled a small silver flask from his pocket, twisted off the cap and took a long swig. The bourbon burned as it slid down his throat. He wiped his mouth with the back of his hand and reached for the envelope inside the safe. Carefully, he opened it, pulled out the two items and placed them on the floor.

The file folder held information about a suspicious fire in Phoenix, and another in Denver that Jane had set herself. According to the report, she was pissed at the guy she was doing so she took his clothes out of the closet, piled then on the balcony, covered them with gasoline and set them ablaze. During his research, Kurt discovered that Jane was quite a little firebug. In her youth, she'd been tossed from two of the finest boarding schools in Europe for starting fires in the garbage chutes.

Kurt's hands shook as he picked up the videotape. On it, investigators would find the home movie of Jane and her latest ride, city firefighter Michael Wells. The cowboy film was no Roy Rogers and Dale Evans family flick. It was hard core porn and Kurt was sure it would bring a pretty penny on the black market.

Michael Wells was propped up on the bed with pillows. Pigging string, tied with two wraps and a half hitch, secured his arms and legs to the four bedposts. He was wearing black ostrich cowboy boots. His genitals were covered with an eight-inch sterling silver belt buckle. The gold letters surrounding the image of a perfect ride spelled out the words Saddle Bronc Champion 1995. There was a blue polka-dot handkerchief tied around his neck. A pale yellow straw cowboy hat resting on his head, and an anxious smile dancing across his face.

"Are you ready to go for a ride cowboy?" Jane's southern drawl asked from the doorway. The sound of cowboy boots on the hardwood floor got louder. Soon, Jane was in the picture. Her long shapely legs were covered with black leather chaps that framed her bare, tanned tight ass like a work of art.

Her long, silky hair hung down her bare back in a single braid. There was a riding crop in her right hand and a braided cotton rope in her left. As she walked towards the bed, she asked, "Do you want to go for a ride Michael? Well, take a deep seat and a far away look because I'm going to give you the ride of your life."

The sound of the telephone shook the image from Kurt's mind. He was about to answer it when he remembered that he was supposed to be at the nursing home with his mother. He let it ring, and quickly put the file folder and the tape back in the envelope. The film would never be released but Kurt knew if it was, Jane's career would be over. He hoped the fire department thought so too when they saw the movie.

In case they didn't, Kurt had a backup plan. He reached into his pants pocket and pulled out the one-page note he'd written earlier. He flipped it open and read it out loud. "If something should happen to me, please investigate the information in this envelope. I believe it will lead you to the person responsible." It was a bold statement and when he was questioned about it later, he'd tell investigators that the evidence spoke for itself.

Kurt went over the speech he'd prepared in his mind: *No, I didn't make the tape. A friend sent it to me. I don't know where he got it. Yes officer, I told Jane about the tape when I received it. Was she mad? She was furious. No officer, I wasn't using the tape to blackmail her. In fact, I was planning on giving it back to her. Why didn't I give it back to her right away? Well, I told her I'd give it to her if she'd go out for dinner with me.*

"Then you were blackmailing her," the officer would say.

I'd hardly call a dinner date blackmail. Yes officer, I realize that this tape could ruin Ms. Phillips' career. I wouldn't want that to happen. I like Jane. I thought she liked me. I just can't understand why she would burn down my apartment.

What makes me think it was Jane? Well I overheard one of the investigators saying that they found traces of lighter fluid. The same brand of lighter fluid Jane uses.

Just in case the fire department didn't believe him, he'd add some fuel to the fire. He pulled a pen from his inside pocket and wrote: *I also believe that Ms. Phillips may have had something to do with the fire death of Michael Wells, the man in this video.*

Kurt folded up the note and set it on top of the envelope. "I've got you now, you bitch."

He closed the door of the safe and spun the dial. Before he stood up, he took another shot of bourbon to steady his nerves. He shoved the flask in his pocket and with the aid of a dresser, pulled himself off the floor. He shuffled to the night table and lit his cigarette fuse. He took a long drag to make sure it was burning before setting it back in the ashtray. At the front door, Kurt stood for a moment and surveyed the room. *If I pull the fire alarm before I leave*, he thought, *the fire department is going to be here before the place really gets going. They may not find the fire trail. But this will help things along.*

He dug into his coat pocket and pulled out a tin of Ronson lighter fluid. He walked into the living room, popped off the red cap, and pointed the can at the sofa. It gave a click when he squeezed it and he smiled as he watched the clear fluid spew from the tip. "Yeah, the fire in living room should be going real nice just about the time the one in the bedroom starts." Kurt lit a match, tossed it on the sofa and watched for only a moment as the fire trail spread across the crushed velvet.

Satisfied that the sofa would burn, he spun around and quickly made his way to the front door. He stepped into the hallway, pulled the door closed and locked it. Before leaving the building, he pulled the fire alarm.

Chapter Six

THE SOUND OF SIRENS woke Sarah Crawford Baker from her drug-induced sleep and for a moment she wasn't sure where she was. Panic set in and her mind flashed back to the fire, and a house that still haunted her memories.

***

Her stepmother was having another party and the noise coming from downstairs had woken her. She slowly sat up and rubbed the sleep from her eyes. *Daddy,* she suddenly thought. *I have to find daddy. I have to talk to him.*

Sarah sprang out of bed and her tiny feet quickly carried her down the long hallway, past the nanny's quarters, and to the top of the stairs. She curled up on the top step and marveled at the sight below as she peered through the white spindles of the winding staircase. The ladies were wearing long, flowing gowns made of silk, taffeta and crepe that came in every color of the rainbow. The men were dressed in black tie and tails. People were talking and laughing and drinking champagne. Scattered throughout the room were the white jackets of the serving staff who offered guests hors d'oeuvres, and refilled their crystal champagne flutes.

Sarah let out a disappointed sigh. She couldn't understand why she hadn't been invited to this gathering. When her mother was alive, she was always invited to her father's parties. But, like last time, and the time before, Janis told her that her father didn't want her there and she'd been ordered to stay in her room.

When her mother was alive, Sarah spent time with her father almost every day. They rode horses and played checkers. They went on picnics down by the river, and he'd even taken her to Europe with him on business. Since her father married Janis, she hardly saw him.

Janis Johnston came into the Crawford household a year before Sarah's mother died. Sarah's father, Jack, hired the attractive young woman to act as a nurse for his wife and a companion for his daughter. He was thrilled when his eight-year old took an instant liking to the young woman. Janis took Sarah everywhere and they soon became steadfast friends. When his wife died, Jack invited Janis to stay on. Six months later, he asked her to marry him.

News of the upcoming wedding upset Sarah, but Janis reassured the young girl that nothing would change. "Sweetheart, your mother has gone to heaven to live with God and I'm sure she wouldn't want you and your daddy to be here in this big, huge house all by yourself," Janis told her.

"She'd want someone to take care of you. Well, that's what I'm going to do. I'm going to take care of you, and your father, just like I've been taking care of you. Nothing will change, I promise. We'll still do all of the things we've been doing. We'll go shopping, and out for lunch. You'll still see your father when he's home from his business trips, and when he's gone, you and I will have as much fun as we do now."

Janis' speech was filled with empty promises that became evident to Sarah the minute her father and stepmother returned from their honeymoon. The new Mrs. Crawford immediately took over as mistress of the manor. She fired the entire housekeeping staff, including Mrs. Pickles, Sarah's nanny of eight years. Janis claimed that Sarah no longer needed a nanny. She claimed she would take care of the little girl as if she was her own flesh and blood, but she hadn't.

Sarah and Janis quit going shopping. They quit going out for lunch. Janis shopped by herself and at lunchtime, she entertained her friends on the terrace of the estate while Sarah ate in the kitchen with the servants.

These days, Sarah rarely saw her father. When he wasn't away on business, Janis made sure she kept him busy. They never ate in the dining room as a family anymore. Sarah was fed, bathed, and in bed before her father came home at eight. She couldn't remember the last time she'd gone on a picnic with her father, or the last time they'd spent more than five minutes alone. Lately, Janis did everything she could to keep the two of them apart.

Sarah's face lit up when her father walked across the foyer. He was a handsome man and someday she would marry someone just like him. He was tall and muscular and when he swept her up in his arms, she felt like a feather. When he held her, she felt safe.

"What are you doing here you little witch? I thought I told you to stay in your room."

Sarah let out a startled gasp and spun around to see her stepmother hovering over her. "Ouch, you're hurting me," she cried out when Janis grabbed her curly auburn hair.

"Well, too bad." She glared down at the child with hate in her eyes. "What are you doing here? Spying on me again, like you were spying on me yesterday?"

"No," Sarah whispered. "I just wanted to see all the pretty dresses."

"Liar." There was a loud crack when Janis' hand came in contact with Sarah's left cheek. "You were here looking for your father, weren't you? You want to find him, and tell him about yesterday, don't you?"

Yesterday, while Sarah was playing in the garden, she heard voices coming from behind the bushes by the pool. She walked closer and listened.

"I can't take much more of this. How much longer are you going to make me wait?"

The deep male voice was familiar to Sarah. *That sounds like Michael*, A beaming smile lit up her face. Michael Wells was Janis' stepbrother and unlike his sister, he was kind.

Since he'd been living at the estate, Michael had taught her how to play tennis and snorkel. He'd taken her for drives in his sports car along the coast highway, and each time, they would stop at the Crab Shell for lunch. He liked her, she was sure of it.

"Be patient," a woman answered. "By next week at this time we'll be sitting with the architects designing a new house."

The familiarity of the female voice startled Sarah. She jumped back, a twig snapped beneath her feet.

"Who's out there?" Janis asked.

"It's nothing, baby. Don't be so paranoid," the male voice casually replied.

"I have to be paranoid," Janis spat. "Lately, that little brat has been watching my every move. All I need is for her to see us together like this. She'll go running to Jack, shoot off her big mouth, and screw up our plans."

"Baby, you worry too much."

This time Sarah was certain the male voice belonged to Michael. She held her breath and listened.

"The kid can't screw up anything. We have everything under control. By tomorrow it will all be over. Now, come here and give me what I came for."

Sarah shook her head in confusion. *Why are Janis and Michael hiding in the bushes?* When her curiosity got the best of her, she gently separated the branches and peered through. Her eyes widened in surprise and she quickly covered her mouth to muffle a horrifying gasp. There was her stepmother lying half-naked in the arms of a man she claimed was a relative. *This isn't right*, she thought. *How could Michael do this to me? How could Janis do this to my father?* Her head started spinning. She suddenly felt sick to her stomach and unexpectedly heaved up her noon meal.

"Who's out there?" Janis asked.

Sarah quickly turned on her heel and without looking back, raced towards the house as fast as her trembling legs would carry her.

***

Janis gave the girl a shake. "I asked you a question, young lady. Are you spying on me again?"

Sarah's eyes dropped to the floor. "No, Janis," she cringed. "I promise." Again, she felt the impact of her stepmother's hand. This time, on her right cheek.

"Well, you're not going to see your father, you little brat! You're not going to see him tonight, tomorrow night, or next week for that matter." Sarah let out a yelp when Janis grabbed her by the arm and pulled her to her feet.

"Sarah, is that you?" Jack Crawford called up from the foot of the stairs.

"Yes, dear. It's us," Janis answered back. "I was just bringing Sarah down to say goodnight."

Jack gave his daughter a big smile and held out his arms. "Come here princess. Come and give me a big bear hug."

Janis pulled her stepdaughter closer and whispered in her ear. "This isn't over, and I'll give you another little piece of advice, kid. If you mention anything to your father about what you saw, or think you saw, yesterday you'll live to regret it." She twisted Sarah's arm. "You got that?"

"Yes," Sarah whimpered.

The minute Janis let go of her, Sarah flew down the stairs and jumped into he father's extended arms. "Daddy, where have you been? I haven't seen you in two days. You didn't come up and tuck me in, and how come I couldn't come to your party?"

Jack gave his daughter a puzzled look. "Well, I'm sorry princess," he apologized. "Janis told me that you weren't feeling well." He raised a questioning brow and turned to his young wife. "I thought you said she was sick?"

"Oh, she is, poor thing," Janis smiled, "but I wanted to bring her down so she could say goodnight to you."

"Well, that was sweet of you, dear." He offered her a smile of appreciation and turning his attention back to his daughter. "Now, let's see what's going on with you, young lady." He gently rested the back of his hand on Sarah's forehead. "Well, you don't seem to have a fever, but your face is sure flushed."

Sarah wanted to tell her father that her face was flushed because it had just come into contact with Janis's hand, but she didn't dare.

"Jack, now be quick," Janis scolded, "and say goodnight to this sweet young thing, so I can get her back to bed before she catches a chill."

He set his daughter on the bottom step and kissed the top of her head. "Now, you run along to bed sweetheart, and if you're feeling better tomorrow, we'll spend the day together."

Sarah looked at her father with pleading eyes. "Daddy, I want you to take me upstairs and tuck me in. Please," she begged.

"Now, Sarah," Janis scolded. "You know that your father has some very important people here tonight that he has to talk to." Her voice was soft and sweet like that of a caring mother. "Be a good girl and come along. You can spend time with you father tomorrow."

When they reached the bedroom, Janis took a firm grip on Sarah's arm. "If you can't stay in your room of your own accord," she spat, "then I guess I'll just have to lock you in like the criminal you are." She pushed the child through the bedroom door. "You better start minding me young lady, because things are going to be changing around here, very soon."

A single tear rolled down Sarah's cheek when the door slammed in her face. She was a prisoner in her own home. She was being isolated from her father, and her stepmother had turned into the wicked witch of the west.

She couldn't help but wonder about the conversation she'd overheard yesterday. What had Michael and Janis been talking about? What did they mean by everything being over in a week?

She picked up Mrs. Pickles; the cat named for her nanny, and curled up on her bed. "I hate that woman," she cried. "Why does daddy keep her here? I thought Janis liked me. I thought she was my friend." Sarah gave the cat an affectionate squeeze, "but she doesn't like anybody but herself. I wish my mommy was here. I wish she didn't die. I wish things could be the way they used to be." She began sobbing and cried herself to sleep.

At three in the morning, Sarah was awakened by the sound of Mrs. Pickles meowing and scratching to get out of the bedroom. She threw back the comforter, jumped out of bed and tiptoed across the floor. When she turned the handle, she was relieved to discover that Janis had unlocked the door. Sometimes, it remained bolted all night. "Do you want to go out Mrs. Pickles?" she asked. "Here you go, kitty."

When Sarah pulled open the bedroom door, her nose was instantly assaulted by the unpleasant odor of smoke. "Daddy, daddy, where are you?" She cried out as she raced down the hallway towards her father's bedroom. As she was about to open the door, someone grabbed her from behind and scooped her off the floor.

"Sarah, we have to get out of here," the male voice told her.

"No. We have to get daddy." She pulled away, and pushed open the door. When she saw her father, a horrified scream erupted from her throat. Jack Crawford was lying face up in the middle of his bed. His body surrounded by the orange glow of flames that were eating the canopy and curtains attached to the solid mahogany bed frame.

"Daddy, daddy, wake up," she yelled.

As she stepped across the threshold, Michael scooped her off the ground. "Sarah, you have to come with me."

She kicked and screamed and fought to break free. "No, Michael, I can't leave my daddy. Let me go."

"Sarah, don't fight me!" Michael urged. "We have to get out of here."

"You can't leave my daddy, Michael," she cried. "You have to save him!"

"Sarah, there is nothing we can do for your daddy. He's already dead."

***

Chapter Seven

THE NOISE COMING FROM the street and the smell of smoke shook Sarah back to reality. She threw back the comforter, rolled out of bed and stumbled to the window to see what was happening. Outside the sky was bright orange from a fire two blocks away. Her palms were cold and clammy and her heart pounded in her chest as she stared out the window and listened to the sirens. "I need a pill."

Sarah quickly turned and raced into the bathroom. She pulled open the medicine cabinet and stared blankly inside. There were as many different shapes and sizes of pill bottles as there were pills. "Which one should I take this time?" She asked out loud.

Sarah's pills came in every color of the rainbow. There were the pale yellow Rivotrill, but they had the least affect. There was the Imovane, but the blue pill was better at night when she couldn't sleep. The Ativan was always good, because it dissolved the quickest; all she had to do was pop it under her tongue. The Xanax came in two colors, peach and lavender. The peach ones were nice, but the lavender ones were the strongest. As a last resort, she could always take a Valium; she still had some left.

After careful deliberation, Sarah chose the lavender Xanax because they usually knocked her out and right now – that was exactly what she needed. She'd been having that dream again. The one where she suddenly found herself dressed in a nurse's uniform and walking into Michael's room.

***

Sarah quietly closed the door behind her. For ten minutes, she stood and stared at the lifeless body of firefighter Michael Wells. His right leg was in a plaster cast from hip to ankle and suspended from the metal track that ran across the top of his bed. His left leg had metal rods protruding from his calf, knee, and thigh.

His chest and both of his arms were wrapped in white sterile dressings. The fingers protruding from under his bandaged hands looked like raw sausages. His face was bright red; his eyes were puffy and swollen. There was a feeding tube coming from his nose and an IV tube running from under the bandages on his arm. "You look pathetic," she laughed. "Maybe now you'll know what my father felt like when the fire ate his body."

Sarah couldn't believe that Michael wasn't dead. She was sure the fire would have killed him. She'd seen fires like that before and firefighters had always perished. Thank God Billy hadn't been seriously injured. His burns would heal. He would recover. Michael Wells never would.

What a load of hogwash Michael's interviews had been after her house caught fire and her father died all those years ago. First, he told the media that he'd rushed into the room, but the flames were too much to take. He hadn't rushed into the room at all. He'd told her that her father was already dead. After the trial, Michael told anyone who would listen that he'd make it up to her by joining the fire department.

He'd make it up to her all right. He'd make it up to her when he was no longer a member of the human race. She didn't have any physical proof that Michael was involved in killing her father and setting the fire, but Janis got what she deserved. She was doing twenty-five to life in a woman's prison.

Sarah slowly made her way to the bed. "Michael, do you know what happened to me after my father died? No, I'm sure you don't," she laughed. "Well, I'm going to tell you." She pulled up a chair and sat down. "After the fire, I was shipped off to a Catholic boarding school. Do you have any idea what it's like in Catholic boarding school? After the trial, I was bounced back and forth between friends and family."

She reached into the pocket of her crisp, white uniform and pulled out a plastic syringe and a small brown vial. "You know Michael, I'm sure the only reason any of my relatives wanted me was because I came with a very, very large bankroll. Thanks to my inheritance, relatives from one end of the country to the other are enjoying new homes and new swimming pools. Do you believe that one of them even bought a Hummer!"

She unscrewed the cap from the brown vial and emptied its yellow powdered contents into the glass of water on the bedside table. She took the glass in her hand and swirled the mixture round and round to dissolve it. "When I was twenty-one, Michael, I wrote the relatives off. I changed my name, my hair, and I set out on a new life. I'd written you off too. Imagine my surprise when I discovered that you and Billy were working at the same fire hall."

Sarah put the glass back on the night table, picked up the syringe and ripped open the sterile packaging. She pulled it from its wrapper and set it beside the glass.

"Speaking of Billy, he's the best thing that ever happened to me. I was never much for dating. I never thought I'd find anyone and then along came Billy." Sarah patted the top of Michael's burned hand. "Oh, and by the way, I never told him that you made a pass at me. It would have only upset him and that wouldn't be right. He had to work with you.

"I've met his parents, Michael, and they love me like I was one of their own. When Billy and I are married, I will be part of their family. Too bad you won't be able to attend the wedding."

Sarah gave Michael a kiss on the forehead. "Just so you know, it won't be the 50mg of Valium that kills you Michael. It will be the small grains of powder that do you in. This concoction will go through your veins like peanut butter. Your blood will thicken as it travels back to you heart, and clot when it reaches your lungs. Within seconds, you'll be dead."

***

Sarah popped the pill in her mouth and washed it down with a drink from the tap. She took two cotton balls from the crystal dish that sat beside the sink and shoved one into each ear as she headed back to the bedroom.

Before crawling into bed, she opened the door of the night table and pulled out one of the three photo albums she kept there. She flipped through the newspaper clippings until she found the article she'd been searching for. It was dated July 12, 1987. The caption read:

PROMINENT RESIDENT DIES IN OVERNIGHT BLAZE

Investigators are blaming the careless disposal of a cigarette for starting a fire on the outskirts of town that killed estate owner Jack Crawford, injured four others, and has left his young daughter homeless.

Fire crews were called to the scene at 3:35 am and arrived to find smoke billowing from the second floor. Firefighters used ladder trucks to reach guests staying at the estate and escorted them to safety, but were unable to save Mr. Crawford.

"I did everything I could to get him out," stated brother-in-law, Michael Wells, who was at the estate attending a party. "I ran into the room, but the flames were just too much to take."

Mrs. Crawford and three other guests were taken to hospital suffering smoke inhalation. Two members of the housekeeping staff were also taken to hospital, treated for their injuries and released.

Sarah felt her eyelids growing heavy and she knew the pill was starting to take effect. She closed the photo album and put it back in the nightstand before crawling under the white duvet. She lay her head on the pillow and closed her eyes.

As she drifted off into a medicated state, she couldn't help but think about Michael Wells and the dream that had been haunting her for months. Michael was dead, but had she killed him? She couldn't remember. In the dream, someone always knocked on the door just as she was about to stick the needle into Michael's IV tube.

Chapter Eight

Six months earlier

AT FIRST GLIMPSE, FIRE Hall No. 5 was unnoticeable. A two-storey gray, concrete building nestled unobtrusively amongst the skyscrapers of the inner city. The building's only identification consisted of the eight-inch brass letters unpretentiously spelling out the business that lay behind its cold cement walls.

Forty-eight hours out of every one hundred and ninety-two, 'A' Platoon's Captain, Ben Taylor, his Lieutenant Pete Metcalfe, the hall's Nozzle Man, Bruce Bradley, First Class Firefighters Garth Hanson and Tony DeMonte, Firefighter Michael Wells and Rookie Firefighter Billy Simpson called No. 5 home. They ate there, slept there, and it was there where they shared the joy and sorrow of a job that was not meant for the weak of body, mind, or soul.

Fire was a living, breathing demon with a mind all its own. It was capable of destroying everything in its path with little or no warning and could change directions with no more than a shift in the wind. A dangerous intruder, fire could suck the life out of its victims in a matter of minutes and injure, or claim the life of at least one North American firefighter every day.

Firefighting could be hazardous to your health and very few people understand why intelligent human beings, capable of doing anything for a living, would choose to eat smoke. Why they wanted to carry eighty pounds of gear into a building where the temperature could escalate from bake to broil in a matter of minutes. Why they risked their own lives.

They did it because they loved the adrenaline rush they

got when the tones sounded and they were called into battle, each different from the last. They did it because they loved the strategy involved in snuffing out the enemy before it had a chance to advance. Like a well-trained football team, when the crew of the offensive line took the field, their purpose was to tackle the opposition in its own end zone.

Most of all, firefighters did it because they loved the warm feeling they got when they saved a life that could have been tragically lost, or saved a building from total destruction. Firefighters were there to help; they were trained to help, and at the sound of every alarm, their training was put to the test.

At forty-nine years old, Ben Taylor, had been a firefighter for fifteen years. He was ruggedly good looking, a real man's man. He stood a proud six-foot two and had a powerful frame. His thick red hair, with its touch of gray, and his warm inviting green eyes made him undeniably attractive to members of the opposite sex.

More than once, Ben had been asked to pose for the Firefighter's 'Hunks and Hose" calendar, a joint venture between the fire department and the local media to raise money for the Burn Treatment Unit. His modeling adventure had earned him the nickname 'Stud Muffin' and his crew teased him constantly.

Ben had been married only once, to a woman he preferred not to discuss, and he had no children, or at least none that he jokingly claimed to know about. When he caught his wife in bed with his business partner, he gave up the mahogany desk, fast cars, world travel, and CEO title of his father's multi-million dollar communication company to join the fire department.

It was Lieutenant Pete Metcalfe's bad grades and tough guy attitude that introduced him to his career in firefighting. He was flunking grade twelve, and causing major problems at home. He'd roughed up a kid in his class, and spent a week in juvenile hall. When he got out, his school counselor told him he had one of two choices. He could join the fire department cadet program, and make up the credits he needed to graduate. Or, on his eighteenth birthday, he'd be sent to jail for assault. The decision was easy. By the time Pete had completed the cadet program, he was hooked.

At fifty-two years old, Nozzle Man Bruce Bradley had been a firefighter since he was nineteen. He'd been asked to write his officer's exam more than once, but always refused. He loved being in the heat of the action and humping hose gave him the opportunity.

First Class Firefighter Tony DeMonte had come from a long line of firefighters. His father and grandfather had both been firefighters and he had two uncles on the job. One in Toronto, and the other in Dallas. Tony signed up right out of high school and his son Allen, had just received an acceptance letter to start training in July.

First Class Firefighter Garth Hanson entered the military when he was eighteen. When given the choice of duties, he chose firefighting. He'd been told that it was a slack-ass job. He'd been told that firefighters spent the majority of time watching television. When he transferred from the army to the city Fire Services, he learned that firefighting was anything but an easy ride.

The hall's youngest member, Probationary Firefighter Billy Simpson, was a Kansas farm boy and the nicest kid you could ever meet. He was polite, respectful of his elders, and never refused to do anything he was asked. When he saw a notice that the volunteer fire department for his county was looking for recruits, he decided to apply. Billy soon discovered that he'd found his calling in life. He contacted the National Firefighters Association, found out who was hiring, and sent out applications. He was thrilled when he was accepted.

Firefighter Michael Wells had come to the Seattle Fire Department from the Mid West. He wasn't a permanent fixture at No. 5, he'd been transferred there on probationary action after being involved in a scandal that made the fire department look like a joke. He'd been partying at the Hose and Hydrant one night when a gorgeous blond walked over and sat down.

"Hi, my name is Robin Brooks. What's yours?"

"Michael Wells," he replied with his sexy smile.

She placed her hand on the inside of his thigh, leaned closer, and whispered in his ear. "So, Michael Wells, are you a real firefighter or just pretending to be one?"

"Honey, I'm as real as they come." He invited her to join him, and discovered during their conversation that she was a photographer for Vogue. She was in town looking for an interesting place to do a photo shoot. Michael suggested his fire hall. He cleared it with the captain at No. 21 and the guys on his crew were thrilled when they discovered they were getting their pictures taken with a beautiful model.

On the day in question, as promised, Robin Brooks, her model, and photographer arrived at the hall at 09:00. The crew had washed the rig and polished the chrome and the apparatus was gleaming. As requested, the boys were dressed in their turnout gear. They wore their black rubber boots and duty hitch minus the jacket and a T-shirt. A bare chest was what Robin Brooks had requested.

While the model was getting ready, Robin positioned the crew on the engine. The junior man was lying on top of the hose bed braced up on his elbow with one leg crossed over the other. She placed two firefighters on the right side of the door into the engine. Both stood on the floor and rested their left foot on the running boards. The lieutenant and Michael stood on the floor with their backs to the door of the engine. The captain was asked to sit in the passenger's seat and look out the window.

The men were told the model would exit through the side door of the rig that was now the main focus of the camera's lens. "Ready boys?" Robin asked. "Everyone say cheese."

When the model jumped out from behind the doors of the big red fire truck, she was wearing nothing but a G-string and a fire helmet. The camera snapped in succession taking picture after picture of her naked body and the expressions on the men's faces. A week later, when the photos appeared on the Fire Chief's desk, he went ballistic. The entire crew was demoted and Michael Wells was transferred to No. 5.

Chapter Nine

SITUATED ON THE BOUNDRY between downtown and suburbia, No. 5 was the smallest of the three inner-city halls. There were days, although few and far between, when the hall sat perfectly still. Its electronic steel doors remaining closed to the hustle and bustle of passersby. The only bells echoing off the cement walls belonged to the telephone. Lately, it seemed to be days like this that had one particular city resident up in arms. After an interview with Lieutenant Mark Turner, the fire department's public information officer, was misconstrued, Ms. Jane Phillips, a columnist at the Tribune newspaper wrote:

'Working for the fire department is like taking a vacation. They sleep when they're on nights, drink coffee when they're on days, and all of them have second jobs'.

Her comments caused quite uproar with the union.

***

"I would like to say something and I think I speak for all of us," Walter Weston, President of Firefighters Union Local 213, began at last month's meeting.

"I don't know where this broad at the newspaper gets off. She seems to have the impression that we don't do anything for a living. She thinks we just sit on our asses all day. Some days we don't leave the hall, but we have to be ready at the drop of a hat. Day or night, during training, fire hall maintenance, inspections, even hall tours, if someone's place catches fire, we're there. If there's an MVA, we usually beat the paramedics to the scene."

You could hear a pin drop as Walter continued to plead his case. "This woman who says we don't do anything all day long, would probably yell the loudest if we knocked over a glass ornament while we were up to our eyeballs in smoke, doing everything possible to make sure her house didn't burn to the ground! She's the same person who'd get choked if we left black footprints on her white carpet while we're making a beeline to her kitchen to put out a grease fire."

Walter leaned into the microphone. "Who does she think cleans up after a water main break, or a lightning storm that dropped half the trees in her neighborhood? Who does she think, sucks up the mess in someone's basement after a flood? If she locked her keys in her car, do you think she'd call a locksmith? Hell no, she'd probably call the fire department."

Walter's voice rose another octave with each sentence. "We aren't just firefighters, we're electricians, gas fitters, carpenters and janitors. We have to learn how to control fuel leaks, deal with hazardous chemicals, building collapses and do high angle rescue. Hell, we even have to learn how to deliver kids! I busted my hump to get here twenty years ago. I started training the day I took this job and I have been training every since."

He slammed his large fists on the podium. "Sit on our asses at the hall? Not bloody likely. We may not hear an alarm all day, we may not hear one for an entire tour, but you can be damn sure we're waiting for it." He paused for only a moment before adding, "I want you all to know that I've taken it upon myself to do something about this bitch."

***

In the last month, the fire department had been inundated with calls, responded to over 1300 of them in the past fourteen days alone. Last week, the department was only one fire away from having to call in off-duty firefighters and spare rigs to handle the workload, and still have coverage in case something else erupted. Very rarely did the city experience three significant fires all at the same time. That day, all hell broke loose.

The destruction began with a major grass fire on the outskirts of town. There was a two-alarm restaurant fire that called out twenty-two firefighters from five different halls. Ben and the crew from No. 5 had been one of them.

At the same time, fires were burning in both ends of the city. In the south, crews were knocking down a blaze in a family dwelling that quickly spread to the homes on either side. In the north, firefighters were tackling a lumberyard fire. Just when things appeared to be calming down, No. 11 station was called to an apartment fire that claimed the lives of three people. The total damage from the fires was estimated to be well over 6.5 million dollars, but the department was sure that those figures would rise after insurance adjusters had completed their investigation.

The biggest fire to date was a three-alarm blaze that raged out of control in the third historical landmark to go up in the past nine months. Shortly after 7:00 am, Rachel McCauley dialed 911 on her cell phone and reported seeing flames coming from the top of St. Jacob's Convent. One by one, stunned commuters pulled to the side of the road and watched in amazement as flames began consuming the roof of the four-storey, red brick structure. Within minutes, a huge plume of thick, black smoke could be seen traveling across the Seattle sky.

The main blaze at St. Jacob's lasted more than five hours and smaller hot spots continued to flare up throughout the day. In the end, it had taken 10 fire halls, 66 firefighters and several hours to knock down the blaze and days to clean up the destruction. The fire was still under investigation, but the fire department was sure they had an arsonist on their hands.

Chapter Ten

JANE PHILLIPS PICKED UP her pad and read her scribbled notes out loud:
"A city man was injured last night when he was overcome by smoke in an apartment fire in the south end. Fire officials believe the man made a desperate attempt to escape. He was found at the front door." The telephone startled her and she quickly dove across the desk to grab it. "Hello, Jane Phillips speaking," she answered in her seductive Texas drawl.

"Jane. It's Kurt."

Her smile faded instantly. *What the hell do you want?* She wondered.

Kurt Roper was a slimy worm, who worked in the newsroom at the Tribune. He was a rude, vulgar little man with greasy hair and a greasy complexion. He was always sober at work, but his complexion displayed every sign of an alcoholic. His nose was swollen and purple. Red veins ran across his cheeks like road maps. His eyes were puffy and blood-shot.

When Kurt spoke with a woman, he never looked at her face. He focused his attention on her chest. It gave Jane the 'heebee-geebees' and she was sure, if given the opportunity, he could easily be a stalker.

Although Jane didn't trust Kurt, she put up with his rude remarks and humored him to get information. He was great at finding skeletons in the fire department's closet. His most impressive piece of dirt to date involved Firefighter Jason Weston, son of Union President Walter Weston. When Kurt discovered that Jason was running off track betting out of a fire hall in the city, he'd passed on the information. The story she'd created was spectacular.

"What do you want Kurt?" Jane asked in annoyance. She was sure he was calling to ask her out again. He'd been trying for months. On his last attempt, he offered to take her to Tahiti and she'd considered it briefly, only because of his bankroll, but the mere thought of having Kurt climb her frame made her sick.

He'd sent her flowers and chocolates. Offered her tickets to the ballet and the opera. Each time she turned him down. She knew that one of these days, she'd have to do something to pay him back.

"Well, Jane," Kurt began. "I have something that might be of interest to you."

She rolled her eyes, and shook her head. "Kurt, look, if you have tickets to the symphony, I told you I was busy next weekend."

"This has nothing to do with the symphony."

"Then, what is it? I have a column to finish."

He let out a disappointed sigh. "Now, now. Is that any way to talk to someone who is about to save your reputation?" There was a momentary pause before he added. "I'd save your ass too, if you'd let me."

"Knock it off," she blurted into the receiver. "I'm not in the mood. Get to the point."

"Well, I was just walking past the fax machine and I happened to see an article that I'm sure you'll be very interested in."

"Why would I be interested in a article coming off the fax machine?" She asked in annoyance, "and what does any of this have to do with me?"

"Well, let me tell yah, sweet cheeks," he took a long drag from his cigarette. "The article is about you, and I must admit, babe, it isn't very flattering."

"What the hell are you talking about Kurt?" she rudely asked.

"You must have really pissed somebody off at the fire department this week," he laughed.

"Will you get to the God damn point," Jane demanded. "I told you I was busy."

Kurt cleared his throat. "As I was saying, before you so rudely interrupted, someone at the fire department doesn't like you, and tomorrow, they're going to show you just how much."

"What are you talking about?"

"Well, tomorrow morning your gonna be on the front page of the paper."

"I am?"

"Yeah Jane, you are, and if the article doesn't get to you, the picture sure will."

"What picture?"

"All in good time my dear. All in good time." He took another drag from his cigarette. "Let me read you the piece first."

Kurt cleared his throat. "Listen to this.

For months, Ms. Phillips has been slamming the very men and women, who protect the City 24/7, our firefighters. September 11th opened the eyes of many people and made them realize that firefighters take their lives into their hands every time they step onto a rig. They never know from one call to the next what awaits around the corner.

Yes, firefighters may drink a lot of coffee and watch a lot of TV, but when they're needed, they respond.

Since the tragic events of 9 -11, when hundreds of New York City firefighters lost their lives in an attempt to save the lives of others, the vast majority of people in this city, and the rest of the country, treat firefighters with a new respect. Unfortunately, Tribune columnist Jane Phillips isn't one of them. Perhaps if she could picture herself in our shoes.

There was a moment of silence. "Is that it?" Jane asked.

"Yeah, for the article. It may not be long, but the picture sure puts it into prospective."

"Fax the article, and the picture, to me right now," she demanded.

"Can't you at least say please?"

"Fine. Please, fax it to me."

Jane tapped her fingers impatiently on her desk as she waited for the fax to roll off the machine. When she saw the picture, she went ballistic. "Those bastards," she yelled into the phone. "How dare they insult me like this!"

The computer-generated photograph portrayed her in full firefighter turnout gear. Her slim frame looked to be three hundred pounds. Her face was covered with soot. She wore a fire helmet, duty coat, hitch and black rubber boots. There was an air tank strapped to her back and a facemask resting on top of her helmet. She had climbing rope over one shoulder, a roll of electrical wire over the other, and a toilet plunger hung from her tool belt. There was a fire hose in her left hand, the 'Jaws of Life' in her right, and a stethoscope dangling from her neck. The caption beneath the picture read:

'Which one of my jobs would you like?'

"The picture isn't very flattering is it Jane?" Kurt chuckled, "Who'd you piss off?"

"Oh, shut up," she spat. "This isn't funny. Who sent it?"

"It doesn't say."

"Who was it faxed to?"

"Bob," Kurt replied.

"Well, don't give it to him. Shred it. If he comes looking for it, tell him you haven't seen it, and ..."

"Not so fast missy," Kurt interrupted. "I'm about to save your ass from a rather embarrassing situation. I think I deserve something in return. Don't you?"

Men are all the same, she thought. *You ask them to do something for you and they all expect something in return.* She rolled her eyes and shook her head. "Fine. What do you want?"

He took a deep breath. "If I do this for you, I want you to promise that you'll have dinner with me, followed by a nightcap at my place. I have some very interesting film I'd like to show you."

"Fine, Kurt, I'll have dinner with you. Now shred the fax."

"Only dinner? Aren't you forgetting something?"

"Yes, if you insist, a night-cap and a movie."

"I don't like your attitude Jane," Kurt firmly stated. "I thought we were friends? Friends aren't supposed to be rude. You, my dear, are being very rude." He let out a grunt. "I'm hanging up now. You can read all about it in the morning paper."

"No, Kurt, wait."

The urgency in her voice made him smile.

Jane took a deep breath and her southern drawl turned honey sweet. "Kurt, I'm sorry," she apologized. "It's been a real stressful week. Forgive me for being so rude. I know we're friends. You've saved my ass more than once, and I do appreciate you giving me a heads up on this." She rolled her eyes. "I'd love to have dinner, and a nightcap with you. Just name the time and place."

"You're not going to bail on me again are you? Like the last time, and the time before that?"

"No, Kurt, I promise. Just let me know where and when and I'll be there."

"You're sure," he asked. "Because if you blow me off again Jane, I may just have to do something about it."

"What's that supposed to mean?"

"What it means is, this time, you better keep your promise."

"I will," she lied.

"Fine, then there's just one more thing."

"What?" She asked impatiently.

"Wear that blue dress you wore to the office Christmas party."

"Why?"

"It really shows off your tits."

She shuttered in disgust. "Fine, I'll wear the blue dress. Now, get rid of the fax."

"Say please."

"Please."

As she heard the paper shred, she let out a sigh of relief and hung up the phone. Her skin crawled just thinking about having to spend an evening in the presence of that grotesque little man, but she'd weasel out of it somehow. She could weasel out of anything.

Jane turned her attention back to the picture and the comments below it. *Who could have done this*, she wondered? From the way it was written she was sure the author had connection to the fire department. If not, they wouldn't be this passionate about their cause.

As she read it over again, a comment in one paragraph kept jumping out at her. "If she could picture herself in our boots." Now, she was positive a firefighter was behind this piece of journalism. The first person who came to mind was Walter Weston. His son, Jason was suspended the day her story broke.

Jane ran into Walter a few days later and he wasn't a happy man. She had been attending her first, firefighters, 'Just For Ladies' an elaborate function put on by the fire department's burn treatment unit to raise money for the Burn Treatment Society. There was food and drink and firefighters; hundreds of them showing off their big, brawny muscles. As far as she was concerned, it had been a worthwhile evening, a real fact finding event, in more ways than one.

Twenty minutes after she walked in the door, she honed in her radar and picked out the gorgeous, brown hair blue-eyed firefighter she planned on taking home with her. She followed him to the bar and stood a few feet away. Twice, she'd tried to talk to him, but each time, some giggly, half-cut female would run up to him and beg him to give her the fire department T-shirt he was wearing.

When he was finally standing alone, Jane struck up a conversation. His name was Michael Wells. He worked at Fire Hall No. 5 on 'A' shift. He gave her a pocket size fire department calendar with his schedule on it, and invited her to come over to the hall for coffee sometime. Jane suggested they not put off till tomorrow what they could do today. She was just about to give him directions to her place when Walter walked over and interrupted their conversation.

"Well, well, well." He glared. "I'm rather surprised to see you here Ms. Phillips."

"It's a free country, Walter," she coldly replied. He took a step towards her and the smell of rum was overpowering.

"I'd of thought that you'd be out scouring the street, like a sewer rat, trying to dig up more dirt on the department," Walter rudely remarked.

"Come on, Walter." Michael took him by the arm. "I think you've had a little too much to drink. Maybe it's time for you to go home and sleep it off."

Walter pulled his arm free, and fixed his cold stare on Michael. "Let me give you a word of warning buddy. Stay away from this woman, she's poison. She'd just as soon ruin your career as write the truth."

Michael flashed Jane a puzzled look. "What's he talking about?"

"I'll tell you what I'm talking about," Walter spat. "If you hang around this broad, she'll ruin your career just like she ruined my son's."

"I didn't ruin your son's career Walter," Jane remarked in a matter of fact tone. "He managed that, all by himself. Now, if you'll excuse me."

As she turned to walk away, Walter grabbed her by the arm. "I'll get you for this."

"Is that a threat, Walter?"

"Take it anyway you want."

***

The willowy blonde shook the incident from her mind. *That encounter was months ago. Surely Walter would've stopped pouting by now.*

She wondered if perhaps the picture and comments had come from the fire department's public information officer, Mark Turner. When she started working for the Tribune, he'd been more than happy to help in anyway he could. After she ran the pictures her college roommate, Vogue photographer Robin Brooks took at fire hall No. 21, he clammed up.

A devious smile swept across Jane's face. Maybe she should take the time to get to know Mark better. She was sure if she could get him alone for an evening, he'd forgive her. Perhaps someday she'd get the chance but until then, she'd see how much mileage she could get out of Michael Wells and that Battalion Chief she'd met at Mayor Wood's birthday dinner.

"Hey, what yah up to?"

Jane jumped at the sound of Michael's voice and turned around. "Jesus Christ Michael, you scared the hell out of me. What are you doing here? I though you'd left already."

Michael reached under her silk nightshirt and wrapped his arms around her tiny waist. "Well, I didn't get lucky last night." He nibbled at her ear. "You were too busy working on your article. So I thought I'd stick around and let you help me out."

She shot him a disgusted look. "Has anyone ever told you that you're a pig?"

"All the time." He pulled her back into her arms. "Come on Jane, I know you want it too."

"Michael, stop it. I'm not in the mood." She freed herself from his grip. "Aren't you suppose to be at work this morning?"

"Yes."

"Then why aren't you?" She asked as she walked out of the kitchen.

Michael followed her to the front door and grabbed her again. "The kid from D shift is covering for me for a couple of hours. I told him I had some business to take care of this morning. Come on Jane, let's take care of business!"

"Michael, will you knock it off. I'm not in the mood. Get your stuff and go to work like a good little firefighter."

"Will I see you later tonight?" He asked.

"Maybe," she told him as she opened the front door. "Goodbye Michael." Jane gave him a push to help him on his way.

"Wait a minute, I have to get my stuff."

"Well, get it and leave. I have work to do."

When Michael was gone, Jane focused her attention back on the fax and the picture she'd just received. "I can't believe someone would do this to me," she announced. "So what if I write the odd nasty article. It's my job for Christ sake. They'll pay for this." She jumped up, grabbed her coat off the back of the chair and headed to the garage to hunt for her supplies.

Chapter Eleven

WHEN THE SHIFT CHANGED at No. 5, the morning conversation was once again, Jane Phillips. "Hey, Ben, did you see the article in the paper this morning by our favorite newspaper reporter?" Bruce asked as he wandered into the fire hall kitchen and directly to the coffeepot.

Ben shook his head. "I haven't even looked at today's paper. I was up all night getting things together for our Safe Kid's program."

"It's only June man! That doesn't happen until October. Not until Halloween."

"I know, but Spokane is getting in on it this year and I have a meeting with their Chief next week." Ben let out a huge yawn. "So, in answer to your question, no I haven't read the article."

"It's about that condo fire last week," Bruce told him. He put down his jelly donut and wiped the white sugary powder from his fingers. "Let me give you the Reader's Digest version." Bruce pulled the paper towards him, cleared his throat and began to read:

"The Fire Department is denying claims that they were slow to respond to a fire which broke out last week in a condo complex in the city's West End.

The blaze damaged three wings of the complex and residents are up in arms, claiming that it took the fire department nearly fifteen minutes to respond."

"That's bullshit!" Garth protested.

Bruce threw down the paper and surveyed the faces of the crew. "I swear to God, that woman hates firefighters."

"Who hates firefighters?" Tony asked as he wandered into the conversation.

"Jane Phillips, that broad from the Tribune newspaper. You know, Michael's girlfriend," Bruce grunted.

"Yeah, she sounds like a dame who worked in Denver," Pete began, "I've got a buddy on the job ..." He paused in mid sentence. "At least, I had a buddy on the job there. He died in a fire, in his own house. Anyway, before Brad died," Pete continued, "he told me that their department was getting jerked around by some dame from one of the TV stations."

"Yeah, she's a real piece of work that one," Garth added.

"Did Turner have anything to say about it?" Ben asked.

Bruce scanned the article looking for the PIO's comments. "Oh, here it is." He adjusted his glasses and continued to read:

"Fire Department Public Information Officer, Mark Turner, stated that firefighters were on scene within four minutes of receiving the 911 call from dispatch."

"That fire was burning long before anyone called the fire department," Pete stated.

Bruce shook his head in agreement and continued reading:

"Some residents and onlookers, who prefer not to have their names mentioned, claim they noticed smoke coming from the building long before the fire department arrived."

"Greg Bishop told me on the phone last night that it took his crew seventeen minutes before they actually started to attack the fire," Tony stated.

"Rookie, here's a question for you," Bruce smiled. "How come the crew didn't attack the fire as soon as they got there?"

Billy cleared his throat. "Because we can't start attacking the flames until we get everyone out of the building."

Tony gave the young man a pat on the back. "Very good Rookie. I see the old man's taught you a few things."

"Who are you callin' old?" Bruce protested.

"What's up guys?" Michael asked as he wandered into the kitchen.

"You're late, Wells."

"Yeah, sorry, Lieutenant. I had an interview with Jane Phillips."

"You what?" Pete spun around and glared at Michael. "Didn't you read the memo about interviews?"

Michael shook his head. "What memo?" He asked.

Last month, after spending an hour at No. 14 fire hall interviewing a rookie about the job, Jane Phillips reported that the captain and his crew had gone to the aid of a pet owner whose iguana had somehow gotten stuck in a basement drainpipe. Members of city council were furious, stating in an interview with her the next day that it was a ridiculous waste of firefighters time, and the city's resources, to go out on pet owner distress calls.

Members of the fire department weren't upset by what city council said, or what Ms. Phillips wrote; they were used to it. What upset them were the comments made by the pet owner himself. He told Ms. Phillips that he'd thought about calling animal control, but that the fire hall was only three blocks from his house. "Besides," he stated, "I figure they needed something to do anyway."

At the end of the article, Miss Phillips added her own personal comments:

If the fire department is responding to such frivolous things and something major erupts, the entire city and everyone in it will be in jeopardy.

Mark Turner reassured city residents that whenever firefighters were out on such calls, they were always ready to respond to any major incident. "We try to avoid these calls by deferring them to Animal Control," he'd told the press, "but if no one else is available, we'll handle it." Turner also told city residents that the fire department wanted people to call them, they encouraged people to call them. In fact, their motto was:

When you don't know who to call, call the fire department.

After the press conference, Turner sent a memo to every fire hall in the city advising that absolutely no one granted interviews but him.

Michael casually strolled to the kitchen counter and poured himself a coffee. "Chill out Lieutenant. It wasn't that type of an interview." A sheepish grin swept across his face. "It was more, up close and personal if you know what I mean."

Pete glared at the firefighter. "Get laid on your own time from now on. That's an order. Now, get out and check the rig."

"Hey Rookie," a voice broke in over the loud speaker. "The soon to be ball and chain is holding on line one for you."

"Kid."

"Yeah, Bruce."

"When you're finished discussing wedding plans with Sarah, get your shit together. We're going out on inspections."

"You better put on your best smile," Michael added.

"Why?" Billy asked.

"Why? Because we're doing inspections in the Bluffs."

"The Bluffs?"

"Yeah, that's where all the divorced cougars live," Michael laughed. "Hook up with one of those broads and you're set for life."

Chapter Twelve

RACHEL MCCAULEY SET HER coffee on the end table and curled up on the couch to read the morning paper. She flipped to the city section and the first article that caught her eye told her about the upcoming firefighters' gala. She pulled her granny glasses from their leather case, set them on the bridge of her nose, and began to read.

City firefighters will soon let their hair down at the upcoming twenty-fifth annual Firefighters Awards Night and Gala. The one-hundred and fifty dollar a plate charity function is dedicated to honor the brave men and women who risk their lives for a living.

Each and every day ordinary citizens call upon firefighters in their most desperate time of need. This year's gala will bring together professional, business, political and other community members to celebrate and recognize those who act selflessly and beyond the call of duty.

The doorbell drew Rachel's attention from the article. She tossed the paper on the walnut coffee table and headed across the ceramic tiled floor to the front foyer. With a long graceful finger, she pushed the intercom button. "May I help you?" She asked.

"Good morning, " the male voice began, "I'm with the fire department."

For a moment her heart caught in her throat and she took a deep breath. "What can I do for you this morning?" She asked.

"Ah, yes Miss. Ah, we're in the neighborhood doing house to house inspections for our smoke detector program. It's a service we provide city residents every six months," the voice continued. "Do you have smoke detectors Miss?"

"Yes," Rachel replied.

"Are they battery operated or hard wired?"

Rachel thought for a moment. She'd never been real handy with construction, but she knew a thing or two about smoke detectors. "I believe they're hard wired," she answered.

"Have they been tested this year?" The firefighter asked her.

"I wouldn't know. I just moved in not too long ago."

"We'd be happy to come in and check them for you. If you like Miss."

"That would be great." Rachel turned the brass handle on the smoked glass front door and the hinges gave a squeak when she pulled it open.

Pete Metcalfe gave her a friendly smile from behind the wrought iron gate on the other side of the courtyard. "We can fix that for you too!"

"Good morning, Lieutenant," she smiled back. "A little WD-40 perhaps?"

"How did you know I was a lieutenant?" Pete asked.

"I can tell by the stripe on your shoulders." When he gave her a puzzled look, she added, "I have friends on the job in Canada."

"Really," he smiled. "Then you should know all about smoke detectors."

"I certainly do." Rachel gave him an inviting smile. "You're welcome to come in and check them anyway if you like." She pressed a button on the intercom and the gate gave a click. "It's unlocked. Just give it a push."

As the men stepped into the courtyard, Rachel's bull mastiff took a firm stance in front of her. A low threatening growl rose in the dog's throat. She reached down and put her hand on his neck. "It's okay Benny," she whispered, "they won't hurt you. I promise. Now go play." The dog gave a woof in reply and trotted out of the room.

"Nice dog," Billy cautiously remarked, "but he seems to have a thing for uniforms."

"Oh, don't worry about Benny," Rachel chuckled. "His bark is much worse than his bite." She stepped back and invited the three men inside.

"Pete, do you want to come back to the rig for a minute," a voice asked from the radio attached to the lieutenant's shoulder.

"I'll be right with you Captain," Pete replied. He gave Rachel a smile. "I'm going to leave you in capable hands. The boys will finish going over the checklist with you, and then have a walk through the house to check the detectors and make sure they all work."

"That will be fine," she smiled back.

Billy cleared his throat. "Where are your smoke detectors located?" He asked. "I'll go check them."

As he turned to walk away, Michael reached out and grabbed him by the arm. "Here." He shoved a clipboard into Billy's chest, "You ask the questions, I'll check the detectors."

What Michael really wanted to do was stay and chat up this gorgeous brunette, but the kid had screwed up twice today and if something happened, it would be his ass on the line. He gave Rachel an inviting smile. "Don't go away. I'll be right back."

I don't believe it, Billy thought to himself as he watched Michael walk away. *The guy's at it again.* At the Fire Department's 'Just for Ladies' Michael had picked up that newspaperwoman Jane Phillips. The two of them had been a hot and heavy item ever since. So hot, in fact, that on their last night shift Billy had caught the two of them going at it in the paramedics' room. Billy shook the image from his mind and pulled a pen from his pocket. "I just have a few more questions to ask you," he blushed.

"Go ahead."

"Do you have a home evacuation plan?"

Rachel's face turned red. "I'm actually embarrassed to say that I don't, but as I mentioned earlier, I just moved in."

"Are your bedroom doors closed at night?"

"Why?" She asked.

"Well, if there was a fire in the house, and say it started at the other end, having your door closed could just save your life," Billy told her with a proud smile.

"Hey, kid," Michael yelled from the hall. "You want to come here for a minute. I need your help with something."

"I'm sorry," Billy apologized. "Will you please excuse me. I'll be right back."

While Billy and Michael went about their business, Rachel made herself comfortable on the sofa and went back to the article she'd been reading. She learned that the money raised from ticket sales and the silent auction at the firefighters' gala would go to the Burn Treatment Unit, the Children's Hospital and the Child Abuse Center. Besides the Medal of Valor, there would be a Citizen's Medal of Honor, a Certificate of Achievement, a Station Citation and a Community Service Award.

Rachel adjusted her glasses and began scanning the article. She was down to the last paragraph when her concentration was interrupted by the sound of a male voice.

"We're all done here Miss," Michael announced from the foyer.

"Oh, great." Rachel put down the paper and walked to the front entrance. "That didn't take long," she smiled, amazed at how quick they'd been. She looked around for the other firefighter. "Where's your partner?"

"He's gone back to the rig," Michael answered as he handed her the clipboard. "Could you just sign this for me, please?"

As Michael watched her autograph the page, he couldn't help but take notice of her shape. He tipped his head slightly and eyed her from top to bottom. She was tall and lean, and although he could only see the outline of her form under the ivory silk robe, his imagination ran wild. When she handed back the clipboard, he held it at his waist to hide his erection.

"Is there anything else you need?" She asked with an enticing smile.

"As a matter of fact, there is," Michael grinned. "Would you mind answering a question for me?"

"If I can."

"Have we ever met before? You look really familiar."

Rachel shook her head. "Oh, I don't think so. I'd never forget a face like yours."

Michael gave her a cocky grin and stuck out his hand. "My name's Michael Wells. What's yours?"

"Rachel McCauley," she replied as their hands met.

Their eye contact was broken by the sound of Pete's voice coming from the radio attached to Michael's shoulder. "Wells, are you ready to go?"

Michael reached up and pushed the button on his radio. "Yeah, Lieutenant. I'll be right with you." He turned his attention back to Rachel. "Are you sure we've never met?" He asked.

"No," she grinned. "I'm positive. I'm sure I'd remember meeting you."

"You mentioned you were new to the city." Michael handed her a card. "Here's my phone number. Give me a call sometime. Maybe I can show you around town."

"Thanks," she smiled, "perhaps I will."

As he turned to walk away Rachel stopped him with a question of her own. "I understand the fire department has some big function coming up"

"Yeah, the firefighters' gala."

"Are you going?" She asked.

"As a matter of fact, I am," he smiled.

"Well, then," she offered him a shy grin. "Maybe I'll see you there."

Michael's face lit up. "Do you have a ticket?"

Rachel shook her head. "No, I just read about it in the paper, and I thought it might be fun."

"This thing is usually sold out three months ahead of time every year," Michael told her. "I doubt very much that you'd even get a ticket."

"It sounds like this gala is a big thing?"

"Biggest party of the year," Michael beamed.

Rachel shrugged her shoulders and let out a disappointed sigh. "Well, I'm sure it would have been fun. Maybe next year."

"Yeah," Michael frowned, "maybe next year." As he opened the door, it dawned on him that perhaps this gorgeous, lanky creature would be interested in going with him and he turned back to face her. "Hey, I happen to have an extra ticket. If you want, I could leave it at the front door for you."

"Thank you, but that really isn't necessary," she smiled. "Besides, I'm sure a good looking guy like you must already have a date."

Michael dropped his head in embarrassment. "No," he lied. "As a matter of fact, I don't." *I'll figure out some way to ditch Jane,* he told himself as he took the card back from Rachel and scribbled something on the back. "Here's my cell number. If you change your mind, give me a call."

"Wells, let's move it," Pete's voice bellowed from the radio.

"Listen, I have to go. If you change your mind about the gala, give me a call." He reached out and touched her on the shoulder. "It was nice meeting you."

"It was nice to meet you too."

When Michael was gone, Rachel went back to the sofa to finish the article she'd been reading. A gasp escaped from her throat when she read the last paragraph.

At this year's gala, Captain Ben Taylor and his crew will receive the community service award for the outstanding work they do with the UNICEF, Safe Kid's Halloween Program.

Ben Taylor, she thought. "No, it couldn't be." The only Ben Taylor she knew was Nichole's ex-husband and she hadn't seen him in years.

Rachel laughed off the thought of Ben being a firefighter and turned the page. There staring back at her, was the familiar face of Fire Captain Ben Taylor, the very same Ben Taylor who'd married her college roommate, Nichole Cook, almost fifteen years ago. Rachel shook her head in disbelief "Ben Taylor, I don't believe it. What in God's name could have ever possessed you to become a firefighter?" She asked out loud.

The last time Rachel saw Ben, he was running his father's company. When she ran into his business partner in Denver five years ago, she discovered that Ben and Nichole had split up. Greg hadn't told her the reason, but she was sure he had something to do with it. He'd slept with everyone else in the wedding party, why not the bride?

She wondered if Ben was still single or if he'd remarried. *Well, there was only one way to find out,* she told herself. In a split second, Rachel made a decision. She picked up the telephone and dialed Michael Wells' cell number.

Chapter Thirteen

FIRE ALARMS WERE AS unpredictable as the winning lottery numbers and when they sounded, firefighters moved. They had to – people's lives depended on it.

The call was received from dispatch at 18:51. Rookie Firefighter Billy Simpson looked disappointedly at the plate of prime rib in front of him. "Well, I guess dinner's on hold tonight," he commented as he pushed back from the table.

Tony and Garth calmly stood up and left the kitchen. As they walked towards the alarm room, they listened carefully as dispatch rattled off the map and grid numbers over the loud speaker.

"Engine Company No. 5, Ladder Company No. 5, please respond. Reported building fire at 1217 Beacon Street. Map 27, Grid 18. Pre-plan 216."

Billy chuckled to himself remembering how he'd reacted the first time he heard the alarm. It had been his first day on the job two months ago. When the tones went off, he was so excited that he hadn't heard a thing dispatch had said. In his enthusiastic effort to be the first on the truck, he sprang from his chair, stumbled over his own feet, and landed face first in the middle of the kitchen floor.

Beet red with embarrassment Billy picked himself up, and charged out to the apparatus floor. He jumped into his hitch, yanked one red suspender over each shoulder and threw on his duty coat. In a hurry to put on his flash hood, the balaclava-like shell firefighters wear over their heads to protect their ears and neck, he ended up with it all twisted and cockeyed.

The men who remained behind stood in the doorway of the apparatus floor pointing fingers and laughing. Billy was the hydrant man and rode the engine. He was raring to go and the engine hadn't even been called. Dispatch had only requested the ladder. When the crew told him to relax, that he wouldn't be going this time, he looked like someone had just shot his dog.

"Come on kid. Let's go."

The sound of Bruce's voice snapped Billy out of his daydream. He stood up and calmly followed his nozzle man from the kitchen. This time he wouldn't run, he knew better.

He'd learned over the past few months to listen to the announcement that followed the bells. He'd learned why firefighters always answer the alarms, or tones as they were called, in a calm orderly fashion. If someone slipped and hurt himself or herself running to respond to an alarm, as Billy had done on his first trip out, it could jeopardize a life by not having the manpower to attend the call.

Billy had discovered over the past month to remain calm at the scene and not rush around like a chicken with its head cut off. He'd learned that when the fire department was calm, and in control, it had a way of calming frantic bystanders.

In the alarm room, Tony grabbed a district map for the engine and Garth grabbed one for the ladder truck. Each man followed the coordinates given by dispatch until they had pinpointed the address.

Ben watched as the printout from dispatch started feeding out of the computer. "1217 Beacon Street. Confirmed building fire." He ripped the paper from the printer and stuck it on the clipboard he'd grabbed off the wall. "We're going in 'hot' boys. Let's move it."

He turned to Garth and Tony. "We'll go down Marine Drive to 56th and turn right. Go across the bridge and hang a left on Dunlop. That should bring us in on the backside and we'll get closer to the building.

"Billy, we'll make the hydrant on the corner of Dunlop and

..." When Ben turned around, he discovered that Billy wasn't in the room. "Where's the Rook?" he asked with a chuckle.

"He's already on the engine," Pete laughed as he picked up the phone on the alarm board and placed it back in its cradle to notify dispatch that the hall had received the call. The action also turned off all of the electrical appliances. Years ago, Fire Hall No. 8 burned to the ground when a pot of grease left on the stove caught fire while the crew was out at a call.

The men headed out to the apparatus floor, jumped into their gear and piled into the trucks. As Tony fired up the engine, Ben picked up the radio. "Dispatch, this is Engine Company No. 5 we're responding to one-two-one-seven Beacon Street."

As the rig pulled out of the hall, the ear-piercing wail of sirens shattered the calm evening air. At 50 miles per hour, the 36-ton vehicle raced to its destination, weaving and dodging its way through the traffic on Marine Drive. Ben lay on the air horn wishing he had the power of Moses and could miraculously part traffic like the Red Sea. Instead, most people paid little or no attention to the urgency of the sirens until the massive vehicles were climbing their bumpers. Some days, traffic could be the most aggravating thing about a call.

In the back of the engine, where he sat with Bruce and Michael, Billy's pulse raced and his heart was pounding like a tom-tom. He was pumped. *It doesn't get much better than this*, he told himself. *Second month in and I've got a live one!*

He closed his eyes and found himself reliving a conversation he'd had earlier with Ben.

***

"Son, when you go to your first 'hot call', the first big one, you'll experience a rush of mixed emotions like you have never experienced in your life. The minute you step onto the rig, everything you learned in training will vanish faster than you can say firefighter.

"You'll forget how to do up your duty coat. You'll forget

how to put on your self-contained-breathing-apparatus. Hell, by the time you get to the call, you'll be so screwed up that you won't remember where to find the hose, let alone how to use it."

"When the engine pulls up beside the hydrant every nerve ending in your body will start to tingle. Your heart will be pounding so hard and fast that you'll think it's going to explode right out of your chest."

"You'll jump off the rig and run to the back because that's what you're supposed to do. But – when you get there and look up and see flames shooting out the windows, and thick, black smoke, belching from the roof, it will scare the shit out of you and you'll freeze in your tracks.

"You'll wonder if the kiss you gave Sarah this afternoon will be the last one you ever give her. You'll wish you hadn't had that stupid fight with your father last night because right now, all you're thinking about is that if you go into that raging inferno, you won't come out and you'll never get the chance to apologize. And for one brief instant Billy, the smell of your mother's homemade bread will fill your nostrils and replace the stench of smoke.

"It's at that instant Rookie, when you're going to ask yourself, 'what the hell am I doing here'? Your palms will start to sweat and you'll want to turn tail and run like a scared jackrabbit, but you won't. Something in your gut won't let you. You're scared shitless and all the way to the call you keep telling yourself that you've forgotten it all, that you can't remember what to do or how to do it.

"But, you know something, the minute you grab hold of the first length of hose everything will come together, the training, the drills, the desire. The reason you joined the department in the first place. You still have fear, but you don't think about it. All you think about is getting inside and doing the job you were trained to do."

***

As the conversation played over in Billy's mind, his eagerness was suddenly plagued with doubt, causing him to shift nervously in his seat. Only three minutes ago he felt indestructible, ready to take on anything. Now, as the sound of sirens roared in his ears, he'd unexpectedly lost his confidence. He'd been to mock-up fires in training, but he was about to come face to face with the real thing and the real thing could kill him.

To a financial planner, fear may have been a changing market. To an electrician, it could have been looking like Duke Nukem after failing to make it to level five, but to twenty-five year old probationary firefighter, Billy Simpson, fear was exactly what the dictionary stated: 'The coming of danger'.

"Scared, Rookie?" Bruce asked with a grin. "If you are, you'd better suck it up because it's too late to turn back now."

Billy swung his head around and stared blankly at Bruce. He hadn't heard a word. He felt the blood drain from his face and he hoped that Bruce and Michael wouldn't notice that he was as white as a ghost. As quietly as he could, he sucked air through his nose and slowly exhaled through his mouth hoping that the exercise would slow his pulse rate and calm his nerves.

He turned and stared out the side window of the engine lost in his own private thoughts. His head was spinning, his stomach churning, and he felt like he was being pulled in a million different directions. *The Captain was right,* he told himself as he debated which was moving faster, his heart or the rig.

He was afraid that if his nervous twitching hadn't already made him look like an idiot, he'd accomplish the mission when they arrived at the call. He'd race into the building and once inside, realize that he'd forgotten the hose. Or, Bruce would ask him to get a pike pole, the harpoon-like object used to tear down ceilings and walls, and he'd forget what it looked like.

At the same time, Billy feared being unable to perform the duties of his job, his body tingled with anticipation at the thrill he was about to face. He would be a hero! He would save a life, save a building, but for every moment of courage, he felt three seconds of doubt. As the truck raced towards the fire, he was beginning to question his abilities.

Chapter Fourteen

SHE MOVED FROM CHICAGO to Atlanta and stayed only long enough to burn down, and collect the insurance money on her father's racing stable. From there, it was on to St. Louis and Boston, then to New York, where she settled in quite nicely.

She loved the nightlife, and had the money to enjoy it. She'd been in the midst of planning something big, a spectacular fire to light up the night sky when September 11th happened. It freaked her out so badly that she decided to move west.

At first, she missed the hustle and bustle of New York as she traveled to smaller cities across the country. She missed the opera and the symphony. She missed the high rollers and the life style she'd grown accustomed to. She finally settled in Kalispell, Montana, and it wasn't long before she found herself enjoying the small town atmosphere.

Kalispell was clean and the people were friendly. She joined a ladies association and hosted the odd tea. She met the mayor, and socialized with members of city council. The nightlife was nothing like New York, but she became a regular at Moose's Saloon and drank beer with the boys every Friday evening.

She'd had a lovely time skiing in Whitefish during the Christmas holidays and one of the girls she'd met on the slopes invited her to a New Year's Eve party. She hadn't planned on going at first but her friend, Suzie, begged and pleaded and she finally gave in. It had been a worthwhile evening, and she was very glad she'd attended.

She met the Chief of the Kalispell Fire Department and after introducing herself as a journalist for Life Magazine, he'd welcomed her into the fire hall with open arms. In the months that followed, she'd gathered valuable information from the firefighters; including the fact that they were sure they had an arsonist on their hands. She knew they did.

***

When she settled in Seattle, she purchased a 2300 square foot condo with a fabulous view of the ocean. It cost her an arm and a leg, but she considered it a gift to herself for not torching anything since she'd left Montana. Tonight, that would all change.

As with every fire, she'd done her homework and she was confident that her plan would go off without a hitch. It would be a good fire. This time she wouldn't use barbecue starter as she'd done when she set Travis Greenwood's apartment on fire in Chicago years ago. This time, she didn't care if arson investigators discovered that the fire had been deliberately set. They'd never figure out who'd set it. In fact, she was sure she'd be doing the owner a favor.

In preparation for the big event, she cased out Brandon's Furniture Store for three weeks. Every morning and every afternoon, she sat in the coffee shop across the street and took notes while pretending to read a book. She recorded the comings and goings of every staff member until she knew their exact schedule. She watched as customers flowed in and out of the store to determine peak traffic hours.

She'd been inside the store several times, mentally measuring the square footage of both floors. During one of her fact-finding missions, she discovered that there were no overhead sprinklers on the second floor. The only fire extinguisher she could find was hanging beside the cash desk. It was for that reason that she chose the pine bedroom suite in the front right corner of the second floor as her point of origin. By the time anyone smelled something burning, and ran upstairs with the extinguisher, the beast would be too hard to tame.

She was sure the fire would be a challenging one to knock down. Firefighters would have a difficult time getting to it. From outside, the building appeared to have windows on the second floor, but they'd been bricked over from the inside years before. Instead of breaking the glass to release the smoke and flames, the firefighters would have to cut a hole in the roof to ventilate. Given the age of the building, she was positive the roof would be layered like a clubhouse sandwich. There would be plywood on top of the rafters, followed by straw, tarpaper and gravel, then another layer of the same.

She knew the firefighters would charge up the stairs, but they'd only make it halfway before they came to a seven-foot landing. At the end of the landing, a solid wall would stop their forward motion. Unable to go ahead, they would have to turn either left or right, and go up another six stairs into the store's individual showrooms.

Once inside their room of choice, a direct line to the seat of the fire would be impossible. There were dining room groupings, living room groupings and bedroom displays. There were bookshelves, wall units and sofa tables. The firefighters would be like rats in a maze. It was perfect!

In order to pull off her plan successfully, she knew she had to choose just the right sales associate, one who wouldn't be at her heels every minute and Stan Brandon, the owner's son, had been perfect. He took a fancy to her the moment he met her. On her first visit, he offered to give her the grand tour, but she smiled politely and told him she preferred to look around on her own. She felt less pressure that way. After several additional visits, some of which were strictly for the sole purpose of flirting with the young man, she had Stanley Brandon eating out of the palm of her hand.

Each Wednesday, Stan's night to close, he locked the front door and turned off the main bank of lights. Then, he took the cash tray from the register and disappeared into the basement. Twenty minutes later, when he reappeared, he put the empty tray back into the register, grabbed his coat, turned on the alarm system, turned off the remaining lights and left. Tonight, things would be different!

"You just take your time," Stan called after her as she

mounted the stairs leading to the second floor. "If you need me, I'll be down here."

As she hit the landing she checked her watch. It was 5:37 pm. *The store closes at six. I have to work fast.* She turned right and headed up the six stairs that would put her on the right side of the store, when looking in from the street. She yanked opened the glass door and stepped into the showroom.

Once inside, she reached into her trench coat and pulled out the three waxed paper ropes she'd constructed earlier in the week. She discovered when she set her last hotel fire, that wax paper made a great fuse. If it was twisted just right, when lit, it would burn along the floor like a fuse of dynamite, only much slower. She knew the waxed paper would leave burn trails along the carpet, but if the whole place perished no one would ever find them.

She quickly unrolled each rope like a firefighter unrolls a hose. With the first one, she moved along the right wall and followed the mental blueprint that would take her through the dining room section, past the desks, and to the front right corner of the showroom. She wove her second fuse through the wall units and entertainment centers down the left wall. With the final fuse, she made her way straight up the middle through a sea of sofas.

In the front corner of the store, she laid the waxed paper ropes one on top of the other, a foot away from the pine bedroom suite that was about to be sacrificed. Next, she threw back the comforter and pulled the mattress towards her. The loud bang it made when it slipped from her hands and hit the floor alerted Stan and she heard him rush to the foot of the stairs.

"Are you okay?" he yelled up.

"Oh, yes," she quickly answered. "I'm just a klutz, that's all. I wasn't paying attention, and I ran into the corner of a sofa."

"Do you need any help?"

"No. Thanks Stan. I've almost made up my mind which bedroom grouping I'm going to go with, so I'll be down in a minute."

She held her breath and listened for his footsteps. When she was sure he'd returned to the cash desk, she pulled a red plastic spray bottle from her pocket and sprayed the top of the box spring with gasoline as if she were refreshing her favorite houseplant. When the liquid had soaked into the material, she sprayed the side of the frame and placed the mattress back on top of the box spring. Knowing from her research that the mattress would be covered with fire retardant protection, she soaked it down as well.

Next, she rolled up a piece of newspaper and tucked one end of it between the box spring and mattress. She placed the other end on top of her waxed paper ropes. The chain reaction would begin when the flames from the waxed paper ignited the newspaper. The newspaper in turn would ignite the box spring. Before long, the gasoline soaked mattress would go up like a Yule log.

She placed the comforter neatly back on the bed and readjusted the newspaper. When she stood back to admire her handiwork, she realized that the matching hutch to the left of the headboard and the two end tables stacked at the foot of the bed would provide more fuel for her little bonfire, so she sprayed them with gasoline as well.

When she was finished, she left the plastic container on a nearby dresser. When it began to melt from the heat, the remaining gas would spill from the container, roll across the top of the wooden furniture, down the sides and eventually ignite along with everything else.

Positive that she reeked of fuel, she pulled a bottle of Obsession perfume from her handbag and gave herself a quick spray. *Obsession, how appropriate*, she chuckled as she tossed the bottle back in her bag.

Before following her paper trail back to the stairs, she took her cell phone from her pocket and dialed her pager number; it would ring in exactly three minutes.

As she made her way down to the main floor, Stan stepped out from behind the cash desk and gave her an anxious smile. "So, did you decide on a new bedroom suite?"

"I've narrowed it down to three," she smiled back, "but I did see a comforter upstairs that would be perfect for my sister's room."

"Which one?" Stan asked.

"The one on the single bed display."

He thought for a minute. "Oh, yeah, the orange and purple one. Right?"

"Yes. I'd like that one, but I need a queen. Do you have it?"

"We sure do," Stan answered with a proud grin. "You know, Dad didn't want me to order those. He said they'd never sell, but you're the third person who's bought one!"

She gave him a congratulatory smile. *Great, maybe daddy will give you a big promotion.*

"I'll just run down to the stock-room and get it," Stan eagerly replied. "Don't go away. I'll be right back."

When she heard his footsteps on the basement stairs, she raced back up to the second floor. She lit the end of each waxed paper rope, and watched for only a moment to make sure they were all burning.

Now, there was only one more thing to do. She had to make sure that there would be no witnesses to her crime. With Stan being a devoted son and employee, she was sure when he realized the store was on fire, he'd try to put the blaze out himself. She had to make sure, if he went upstairs he wouldn't come back down. She couldn't afford to have Stan telling the arson investigators who his last customer had been.

In the room where her fire would start, she pushed a glass end table against the partition wall and attached a piece of wire to one of the legs. She stretched the wire across the floor and attached the other end to the leg of a dining room table.

In the opposite showroom, she wrapped the wire around the leg of a wall unit, stretched it across the floor and attached the other end to a nail protruding from the partition wall. No matter which way Stan turned at the top of the stairs, he'd only make it ten feet before the wire tripped him. She hoped her little booby trap would also capture Michael Wells. She knew he'd be at the call. The fire was in No. 5's district.

Michael was becoming a royal pain in the ass. Last week he'd arrived at her place unannounced and invited himself in. She told him it wasn't a good time, but he insisted. For the first hour, Michael was a complete gentleman. After a couple of drinks, he turned into her Uncle Henry.

"Oh, come on baby. You want it, I know you do."

She'd pushed him away and told him she wasn't interested, but that hadn't stopped him; just like it hadn't stopped Henry or Travis Greenwood or that firefighter in Denver.

Well, if Michael wanted it, she'd give it to him. She'd give it to him like he'd never had it before and when she was finished, she'd kill him just like she'd killed the others.

***

She knew by the time the crew from Fire Hall No. 5 arrived at Brandon's Furniture Store the smoke inside the building would be so thick you could cut it with a knife. Firefighters wouldn't see her trip wire until it was too late. She quickly surveyed the room one more time and checked her watch. "Perfect. It's all about the timing."

With a satisfied smile on her face, she headed down the stairs. By the time she reached the basement door, her pager was going off. "Stan, I have to leave," she yelled down to him. "I've just been paged. I'll be back in the morning to pick up the comforter."

Stan called after her as he ran up the stairs. By the time he reached the main part of the store, she was gone. He let out a disappointed sigh. He had hoped that she'd stick around and they could go out for a drink. He was sure she liked him; he could tell, by the come-hither looks she always flashed his way. *Oh well*, he thought. *Maybe when she's here tomorrow, I'll ask her out for dinner.* Satisfied with his decision, Stan walked to the front door and locked it before taking the cash drawer from the register and heading to the basement.

Twenty minutes later when he came up from the basement, Stan thought he smelled smoke, but he paid it little attention and went to the back door to lock it. When he returned to the showroom, there was a haze in the air and the stench was now too strong to ignore.

He quickly ran behind the cash desk to check the garbage can, but found nothing. Next, he raced to the fuse panel and looked inside, still nothing. He hurried around the store lifting washing machine lids and opening fridge doors. When he noticed smoke oozing down from the second floor, he ran back to the cash desk and grabbed the fire extinguisher.

Stan raced up into the smoke. When he reached the landing, he took the stairs to his right two at a time. He pushed his way through the glass door and turned towards the front of the store. "Holy shit!" he exclaimed. "Fire!"

The front corner of the showroom was burning. Flames were attaching themselves to the surrounding walls on either side of a pine bedroom suite. Stan tightened his grip on the extinguisher and headed towards the fire. He'd taken no more than ten steps when something grabbed at his ankle. He heard a loud crack and his head exploded in pain when it hit the corner of the glass table. Within seconds all was black.

Chapter Fifteen

SIX MINUTES FROM THE time the call was received at the hall, Engine Company No. 5 was on scene. "Let's hustle, Rookie," Bruce announced.

Billy felt a fist punch him in the shoulder and he shook his head, not sure for a moment where he was. He'd been so lost in his own emotional battle that he hadn't even noticed when the rig came to a grinding halt in front of the hydrant.

"Kid, are you going to make the hydrant?" Bruce asked. "Or, do you think the hose is going to run over there all by itself?"

Billy took a deep breath, opened the door, and jumped from the rig. When his feet hit the ground, he went weak in the knees and stumbled. He felt the bile rise in his throat and swallowed hard to force the foul taste back from where it had come. Right now, he would have given anything to be anywhere but here.

At the back of the rig, he swung open locker No. 8 and grabbed the hydrant bag. He pulled a five-inch hose line from the hose bed, threw the end of it over his shoulder, and raced to the red fire hydrant.

First, he wrapped the end of the hose around the metal waterspout so that when Tony pulled away with the engine to start laying lines, he wouldn't take the hose with him. Next, he used his hydrant key and quickly loosened the steamer cap at the front of the hydrant. He attached the hydrant adapter, threaded the port and connected the hose. When he got the okay from Tony, he turned on the water. He stood up, grabbed the hose line at the hydrant and followed it back to the truck. Every one hundred feet, he stopped to check the connections.

When Billy arrived back at the engine he wasn't surprised to see that spectators had gathered for blocks. He'd been told that it wasn't uncommon for people to chase the rigs down the street, or follow the sound of the sirens. He watched in amazement as the gathering crowd frantically waved and pointed towards the smoke coming from the front door of Brandon's Furniture Store.

It's show time folks, he told himself as he took a deep breath to suck in his fear and prepare for battle. Quickly, and as calmly as his nerves would allow, he moved to a side locker and grabbed his equipment. He strapped on his air tank and made his way to the cab to get his orders from Ben. "Where is everybody, Captain?" he asked.

"Garth had trouble getting the ladder started. They should be here any minute."

"Where's Bruce and Michael?"

"They've taken a hose line and gone in. There's a chance the owner's kid is somewhere in the building. According to the other shop owners, the last thing he does before he leaves at night is turn off the lights. They were still on when we pulled up."

The sound of Bruce's voice coming from the radio clipped to the dashboard of the engine interrupted their conversation. "Ben, Wells and I have come halfway up the stairs. There's a landing and more stairs going up on both sides." Bruce advised. "We have extremely high volumes of smoke. We have poor visibility down low. No visibility and high temperatures up top. We're staying low and doing a right hand search."

"Roger." Ben replied.

"Captain, do you want me to go in and help?" Billy asked, anxious to get in on the action.

Ben shook his head. "I'm not letting you in there alone. Pete and Garth will be here any minute. You can go in with them."

"Captain," Bruce's voice broke in over the radio. "We found a body. I think it might be the owner's kid."

"Can you guys get the body out by yourselves?" Ben asked.

"Yeah, we can handle it. He's not that big."

Chapter Sixteen

BRUCE HAD NO WAY of knowing if the person he was about to rescue was dead or alive. It was too hot to take his gloves off and check. He'd have to get him outside before he'd know for sure. The casualty had a nasty gash on his head and it looked like he'd lost a lot of blood. From the amount of smoke in the air, Bruce was sure the kid's lungs were fried.

He pulled Stan's upper body off the floor and propped him against the wall. When he tried to push the glass end table out of the way, something stopped it. Bruce ran his gloved hand across the top and down the sides of the table. He found a piece of wire attached to one of the legs, and followed it across the floor. The other end was attached to the leg of a dining room table. *Strange,* he thought. *This is something Heather Kennedy's gonna want to know.* He filed the information for future reference and went back to work.

Through the thick smoke, Bruce could see the orange glow of the fire and he knew they'd have to move fast. "Wells, I'll take him around the middle. You grab his feet," Bruce yelled over his shoulder. He pulled Stan away from the wall and grabbed him under the arms. "Wells lets move it. We haven't got all day for Christ sake! It's getting bloody hot in here."

When Bruce turned around, he discovered he was by himself. Michael had vanished. "Son of a bitch." He put Stan's lifeless body on the floor and reached for the button on his radio. "Ben, I've lost Wells. He was right behind me coming up the stairs, but I don't know where the hell he is now. I turned around and he was gone."

"Billy and I will grab a hose line and be right in," Ben quickly answered. "Do you need help with the body?"

"No, I'll be okay. I'm pretty close to the stairs. I'll meet you on the landing."

"Ten-four."

Bruce grabbed Stan under the arms, pulled him up off the floor, and started dragging his lifeless body backward towards the stairs. *Fireman's lift my ass,* he thought to himself. *Anyone who's done this knows it's impossible to sling someone over your shoulder when you're wearing an air tank.*

He stopped for a moment to catch his breath and the sound of Darth Vader echoed in his ears as he sucked air through his regulator. He hoped that when he got to the landing, he'd find Michael waiting for him. If the firefighter had gone down somewhere in the building, his personal alarm system would be going off. The only sound Bruce could hear through the smoke was the roar of the fire.

Chapter Seventeen

BEN PICKED UP THE radio on the dashboard of the engine. "Dispatch, this is No. 5 command. We have a firefighter missing in the building. I'm calling a second alarm and relinquishing command to the incoming engine. My Rookie and I are going inside."

"Engine Company No. 5, this is dispatch. We copy your transmission. No. 17 will take command. Dispatch out."

"You ready Rookie?" Ben asked.

Billy felt his heart pounding in his chest. This was it. This was the big one that would initiate him into the fire department. When he met his classmates at the 'Hose & Hydrant' tomorrow night, he'd finally have something exciting to tell them. Every member of his graduating class had experienced the 'Red Devil' first hand. Now, it was his turn.

He gave Ben a quick salute and pulled his facemask into place. He closed the valve on his air cylinder to bleed the lines and watched as the gauge dropped to zero. When the warning whistle stopped and the air flow quit, he took a quick breath to seal the mask tightly against his face, then turned on his air cylinder and inhaled through his regulator to make sure the air was flowing. He checked his gauge. It indicated that he had forty-five minutes of air in his tank. *This will be over by then*, he reassured himself as he followed Ben across the street.

When the two men crossed the threshold of Brandon's Furniture Store, Billy froze in his tracks. For a long moment he stood in awe, mesmerized by the eerie sight before him. He'd expected smoke, but what he now saw had him shaking his head in disbelief. The interior of the store looked like it had been cut in half. From the floor to his shoulders, the room was perfectly clear. From there up, a heavy cloud of light gray smoke hung in the air and filled the room like English morning fog. *This is weird,* he thought. *I don't remember seeing anything like this in training.*

"You ready, kid?" Ben asked.

Billy shook his head in response, took a deep breath to calm his nerves and got down on all fours. He flung the hose line over his shoulder and followed Ben towards the stairs.

The building was black with smoke and along with the obstruction of his mask, Billy couldn't see more than a foot in front of him. With his eyes wide open, he was virtually blind. As he felt his way through the darkness his sense of touch was hampered by the thick Nomex gloves he wore to protect his hands. His flash hood and the flaps from inside his helmet that protected his ears and neck from the extreme heat impaired his hearing. He could smell nothing but the stale air he sucked from the canister strapped to his back.

By the time he reached the foot of the stairs, his heart pounded in his throat and a feeling of anxiety engulfed him like the thick blanket of smoke. All around he could hear evidence of the fire's raging anger. Wood snapped and popped like the twigs of a moisture-starved tree. Timbers crashed onto the floor above. He took a tighter grip on the hose, swallowed his fear, and began inching upward behind Ben.

When they met Bruce on the landing, Ben stopped and put down the hose. "Do you have any idea where Wells may have gone?" Ben yelled through his mask.

"The only way he could have gone was left," Bruce yelled back. "I can't hear his pal going off, so he must still be on the move."

Ben pushed the mike button on his radio. "Tony, what's the status on the ladder?" He asked.

"I can see them coming up the street now."

"Ten-four. When they get here, send them in. Bruce is on his way down with the body. I'm leaving Billy on the landing, taking the line and doing a left-hand search. Bruce is pretty sure that's the only way Wells could have gone."

Ben turned around to face his rookie. "I want you to stay here and keep feeding me the line. Wait for Pete and Garth. We'll stay in radio contact."

Billy shook his head in confusion. He could barely make out a word Ben was saying. With the obstruction of his mask and the roar of the fire, everything was coming out muffled. He pointed to his ear and shook his head. "What did you say Captain?" he yelled. "I can't understand you."

"You stay here and wait for Garth and Peter." Ben shouted over his shoulder as he disappeared into the smoke.

Billy's body started trembling. He'd never been in a fire before, and now he was in one alone. *I'm going to end up like Heather*, he told himself. His mind flashed back to a training lecture only three months ago where he was sure they were told to always stay together.

***

Chief Training Officer, John Kennedy, was a twenty-nine year veteran of the Fire Department. The proud father of two, who had both made it through twelve grueling weeks at the Fire Training Academy, opened his lecture on 'team work', with the same speech, and the same slide presentation he'd used since first becoming an instructor. He claimed it packed more power to the punch.

"Ladies and gentlemen," he smiled. "The first thing we are going to burn into your brain today is that firefighters work on the buddy system. You're not here as individuals. You're here as part of a team. As part of that team, we always stay together. We stay together so we can watch each other's back and make sure nothing happens. You see, if you don't stay with your partner, there's a chance that one of you may end up trapped. There's a chance that one of you might end up dead!"

When the whispers in the classroom stopped and a hush fell over the audience, a fatherly smile came to John's face and he leaned into the podium. "But, first, let's talk about why you're here." He stared into the eyes of his eager students. "I'm sure, there are some of you who've dreamt about being a firefighter all your life." He paused for a moment allowing the eager recruits to briefly re-live their childhood memories. It never ceased to amaze him how every rookie, in every class, got the same stupefied look on their face.

"And, here you are," he grinned. "I'm sure that your parents are very proud of you. In fact, if they're anything like I was with my kids, they've probably been bragging about you for months. Right?" Glowing smiles erupted on the faces in front of him.

John stepped out from behind the podium and continued his speech with the energy and enthusiasm of a football coach preparing his team for the playing field. "I'll bet you can't wait to get to your first 'hot call', your first live fire! You can't wait to rush in and rescue your first victim!" As he watched the sea of faces before him, he knew he was getting them revved up. He could tell by the desire he saw in their eyes.

"Now, I'm going to ask all of you to be really honest with yourself. A moment of truth you might say." He watched as the smiles in front of him faded. "I'll bet there isn't one of you who hasn't pictured yourself as first man inside at the scene." He began drawing a mental picture for his students. "You've all visualized your face splashed across the front page of the morning paper. 'Brave firefighter battles the odds to rescue trapped victim and emerges as a hero'."

As the words left John's mouth, he scanned the room searching for the faces of the ones who wanted to be heroes, the ones that were buying into his scenario; the 'freelancers'. He knew who they were, he could tell by their expressions, the smart-ass-smirks told him these people could be dangerous, not only to themselves, but also to their crew.

"Picture this," John began. "You're at your first fire. You've been through training. You know what you're doing. Right?" Heads bobbed up and down in reply. "You can take care of yourself. Right?"

"Right," the class answered in unison.

As John watched the beaming smiles get bigger and bigger, he knew he had them right where he wanted them. When he was sure that every one of his students were picturing themselves on the front page of the paper, he took a deep breath and yelled with the authority of a drill sergeant. " Well, lose the attitude right here and right now people, or find yourself another job! Here, we don't work alone! Here, we don't, and I repeat, don't, freelance! Here, we work as a team!"

John couldn't help but chuckle as he watched their jaws hit the floor. "Now, I'm going to show you why you never leave your partner. Why? If you'll pardon the expression, you stick to him like shit to a blanket."

When the room was dark and the only sound to be heard was the hum of the slide projector, John cleared his throat and prepared for the slide presentation that never seemed to get any easier. "Take a good, long look, people, because this is what happened to a rookie firefighter their first month on the job."

John swallowed the lump in his throat and hit the projection button. As the first slide was exposed in living color, three recruits left the room, all with their hands over their mouths. "This picture was taken at the hospital immediately following the fire," John announced. "As you can see, the victim suffered burns to well over sixty percent of their body."

Although the incident happened years earlier, the horror of it was still fresh in John's mind and he had to take a deep breath before continuing. "You'll notice that the intense heat from the fire has removed both the first and second layers of skin from the shoulders to the waist."

In the second slide, the firefighter was wrapped in flamazine dressings from the knees up. The unrecognizable face was red and swollen. The eyebrows were gone and the blonde hair was singed almost to the scalp.

"Christ, man, that must have hurt," a smart-ass student yelled from the back of the room.

"Actually, it did," John answered. "This rookie endured excruciating pain in a fight for survival."

"Are you telling us Sir, that this person actually survived?"

"Yes, they did."

A broad smile lit up John's face when he hit the button to reveal the next slide. "This picture was taken in the Caribbean six months ago," he proudly announced. John had taken the picture himself and it was the latest to be added to his collection. Now identifiable, the young woman in the photograph was beautiful. She had a high forehead and prominent cheekbones. Her eyes were deep blue and surrounded by long lashes. Thick blonde hair fell loosely past her shoulders and her inviting smile displayed pearly white teeth. She had an attractive figure and wore a two-piece navy blue bathing suit.

With the face of an angel, the female firefighter could have easily been a fashion model, if not for the grotesquely disfigured skin that covered three quarters of her body. Her upper torso was severely scarred and showed evidence of several skin grafts, some of which hadn't been successful. But, when covered from the neck down, she looked no different than any other attractive young woman her age.

"Oh, my God! How old is she?" someone asked.

"How did it happen?" another questioned.

"Is she still on the fire department?" a voice inquired.

"In answer to your questions," John smiled. "She's thirty now. It happened when she was a rookie with the Chicago Fire Department. We'll get into how it happened as we go through training, and yes, she's still on the job. As a matter of fact, she works in our arson division."

"Sir, you talk about her like you know her. Was she one of your students?"

"No," John replied. "She's my daughter, Heather."

There was a long silent pause before someone asked, "Was she the only one hurt?"

John shook his head. "No. No, she wasn't. One of her classmates died."

"Were they in the fire together?"

Again John shook his head. "No, they weren't. Firefighter

Greenwood wasn't working that night. The original fire started in his apartment. He died in bed."

***

Chapter Eighteen

MICHAEL KNEW THE RULES, they said that you always stayed with your partner, but when Bruce took the stairs to the right, he took the ones to the left. He made a bold decision leaving the hose line to venture out on his own, but the sooner he found the body, the sooner he could get back to the hall. With any luck, in time to watch Judge Judy.

He hated going to fires. In fact, he hated his job. He'd only joined the fire department out of guilt and peer pressure. The guilt was because he'd let Janis talk him into helping her with her stupid little plan. In the beginning, he had no idea it would lead to murder.

He'd met Janis Johnson in Mexico and after spending seven days screwing their brains out she took him home and introduced him as her stepbrother. Janis's much older husband Jack Crawford took a shine to him and invited him to stay on.

"Michael, you'd be doing me a great favor if you would stay here when I'm out of town and look after your sister and my daughter. In fact, why don't you just move in."

It had been one sweet deal. He was given a sports car to drive and an apartment of his own above the garage. He dined in the finest restaurants, drank the best champagne, and never paid for any of it. When the old man was away, he paid Michael a thousand bucks a week to take care of Janis and the kid. Yes, it had been a sweet deal. He was getting fed and fucked and all for free. Then, the stupid bitch had to go and get greedy on him.

"Michael, why have a little, when you can have a lot?"

Janis told him her plan was fool proof. Jack would be out of the picture and the kid would get blamed for the fire. They'd get a new house, a shit load of cash, and live like royalty for the rest of their lives. She told him he'd come out of the whole thing smelling like a rose.

Unfortunately for Janis, her little plan backfired. When she was arrested on suspicion of murder, she promised him half a million bucks if he'd keep his mouth shut. When the money didn't arrive, he sang like a canary.

The peer pressure to become a firefighter came after the trial. As the cameras watched the little girl being taken away on the hand of an uncle, a reporter stuck a microphone in his face and asked: "Will you ever be able to do anything to make up for this child's loss?"

When Michael heard someone mention that he should join the fire department, he jumped at the positive press. "Actually," he smiled, "I've decided to join the fire department. I couldn't save her father's life, but perhaps I'll be able to save others."

Michael became a firefighter and a month into the job, he wished he hadn't. He hated firefighting. It was a filthy, dirty job that he wouldn't give to a monkey. Salvage and overhaul was a royal pain in the ass and his back ached for days afterward.

He hated the grunt work involved with his job, and there were days when he was bored stupid, but the pay was good. He'd even get a pension if he hung in long enough. The hours weren't bad either. Four days on and four days off to pursue other interests.

The biggest advantage of his firefighting career was never being without female companionship. Women swarmed to him like flies to honey. Jane Phillips had latched on to him and he knew that Rachel McCauley wanted him too.

Maybe when he was finished with Rachel, he'd move on to Billy's little girlfriend, Sarah Baker. She was cute and she reminded him of someone he used to know. So what if she was engaged. That hadn't stopped him in the past, why should it stop him now?

Michael put the thought out of his mind, turned left, and moved blindly through the smoke filled room. He'd crawled ahead no more than five feet when his shoulder hit something solid. He ran his gloved hand up and across the object, estimating it to be three feet wide. He moved his left hand around to the front. There were knobs and handles and cubbyholes. *Wall unit,* he told himself.

He pulled himself to his knees, and moved sideways feeling the piece of furniture as he went. When he came to the end of it, he got back down on all fours and made a quarter turn left. Slowly, he began inching forward through the smoke.

Michael knew he should turn around and go back. He didn't have a hose line, and he was sure that Bruce was probably pissed at him for taking off on his own. Finding the kid was going to be a crapshoot anyway. The smoke was so thick he could barely see his own hand in front of his face, let alone find a body. Besides, if the kid was still inside, he had to be dead by now. *Enough of this shit,* he told himself. *I'm getting out of here.*

Michael turned around and reached out with his left arm. When he moved ahead, something grabbed at his right knee and he gave his leg a quick jerk. He felt both legs snap like twigs only moments before his body collapsed under the weight of the oak bookcase.

Chapter Nineteen

THE SOUND OF SOMETHING crashing to the floor above him snapped Billy back to reality. His chest tightened and he took slow, controlled breaths until he felt his heart rate slow down. This may have started out all fun and games, but in his mind the party was over.

For the first time since entering the building, Billy noticed the smoke changing color. When he first walked through the front door it was grayish white, now it was turning grayish green. Everything was closing in around him and he was getting spooked.

The fire was burning hotter now and the temperature inside the building was rapidly escalating. Inside his duty gear, Billy felt like he'd put on six layers of winter clothes and gone to work in a steel mill. The heat was taking its toll and Billy was soaked to the skin. Sweat stung his eyes as it ran from his forehead. Without thinking, he reached up to wipe the perspiration from his brow, but the air mask he wore to protect his face and allow him to breathe stopped his gloved hand. Without the mask, the heat from the air alone would singe his lungs in a matter of seconds.

Billy wondered where Ben was and decided to go investigate. When he looked to his right and saw the hose line sticking out from the glass door he decided to grab it. He crawled up the six stairs, pushed open the door, and rose to his full height of six foot two. Much to his surprise, he could see images through the haze and he gave a sigh of relief. *Good, this will be over soon.*

As he bent down to pick up the hose line, an eerie feeling crept through his body and the hair stood up on the back of his neck. Something wasn't right, he could feel it. There was a strange hissing sound in the air and he was sure the temperature had gone up twenty degrees in the last two minutes.

Suddenly, without warning, the room reached its flashpoint and the ceiling burst into flames. Before Rookie Firefighter Billy Simpson had a chance to blink, a bright orange fireball came out of nowhere. It hit him square in the chest with the power of a linebacker and blew him backward off the stairs.

As he flew through the air, his whole life flashed before him. *You idiot*, he told himself. *You could have done so many things with your life and now you're going to die. This was a really stupid ass career choice!*

He saw the faces of his mother and father and he was saddened now that they would never have grandchildren. He thought about Sarah and he wished he would have run off and married her when he'd had the chance. *Maybe, it's better this way*, he told himself. *If we were married, tomorrow, she'd be a widow.*

In Billy's mind, his young life had been wasted. He was 25 years old; he planned on living to be at least 90, or maybe even 100, like his grandfather. There would never be another Christmas with his family. No more fishing trips with his buddies. No more anything – life as he knew it was about to come to an abrupt end.

A million things flashed through Billy's mind on his two-second flight through time and space. He hit the ground hard and landed backwards on his air tank. He let out a pain-racked groan and tried desperately to catch his breath. His head was pounding and his body felt like it was on fire, but the smell of stale air from the canister strapped to his back told him that he was still alive.

A funny thing crossed his mind then and he couldn't help but laugh. *Now, I know what it means to have the shit scared out of you!* He'd been so frightened when he saw the ball of fire coming at him that he was sure he'd soiled himself.

Billy's strange sense of humor made him realize that he was still in the land of the living. His attitude took an abrupt about-face and he quit feeling sorry for himself. Suddenly, he had the strength of ten men. Some unknown force took over his body and with every fiber of his being he craved the desire to live. He could taste it in his mouth and feel it in his bones. He wanted to live; he had to live; he was going to live. *I'm not going to let the 'beast' take me down. I'll beat it. I have to.*

Billy made up his mind, right then and there, that one way or another, he wasn't going to die in this building. He had too much to live for. His career had only just begun and he wasn't about to let it end like this. He planned on retiring as a captain, maybe even the chief.

He loved Sarah Baker, he was sure of that now. So what if she had ghosts haunting her from the past; something in her childhood that caused the nightmares. They'd go to counseling and together work through her fears. If Sarah wanted a big wedding on Christmas Eve, then that's what he'd give her. He'd work two jobs if he had to, and on December 24th at 8:01 pm, he'd make her his bride.

Billy knew he had to plan an escape route, but he lay perfectly still for a moment afraid to move. Afraid of what would happen to him if he couldn't. Cautiously, he did a physical check to ensure that he still had all of his body parts. He moved his right leg, then his left. *The bottom half works*, he told himself. He wiggled his fingers, bent his wrist and lifted his arms. *The top half seems okay.*

He was sure there'd been a flashover, but he had no idea how much structural damage it had caused. All he knew for sure, was that he had to get out and fast. He slowly rolled over onto his stomach and with trembling hands blindly felt his way through the smoke. When he was confident that the floor around him was stable, he crawled forward on his belly searching for the stairs that would take him back to the main floor and out the front door.

Billy knew that if Training Officer Derek Roberts were here he'd be getting a piece of the British instructor's attitude. The tongue-lashing he got during SCBA training suddenly flashed through his mind.

"Mr. Simpson," Roberts yelled. "What the hell do you think you're doing, mate? If you crawl down here like that," Roberts got down on his belly and began imitating Billy's action, "and you get to the end of whatever it is your crawling on, and there's a six-foot drop that you don't know about, and you're reaching way out there with your arms, and you're flopping around there like a fish, and all of a sudden there's nothing in front of you, what do you think is going to happen to you, mate? I'll tell you what's going to happen. The weight of your air tank will pull you right over the edge and you'll be dead! That's what will happen. Now, get your head out of your ass and do it properly."

As Roberts' words rang in his ears, Billy rolled over and spun himself around so his legs were in front of him. He slowly sat up and began inching forward on his butt. Gingerly, he searched for the staircase hoping desperately that it would still be there. When his left foot dropped eight inches and hit something solid, he was sure he'd found it.

Billy took a deep breath and cautiously began inching downwards on his butt one step at a time. When he was confident that the structure would support his two hundred and thirty pounds of pure muscle, he stood up and made a beeline for the nearest available exit. Downward he raced two steps as fast as his legs would carry him.

When Rookie Firefighter Billy Simpson burst through the front doors of the furniture store to escape the clutches of the burning building, his helmet and gloves were smoldering and a cloud of smoke circled his head like a halo.

The heat from the flashover had melted Billy's helmet badge to the top of his helmet, burned his neck on either side of his duty coat, burned part of his uniform, and melted his gloves onto his hands. His adrenaline had kicked into high gear and he felt no pain.

"He's out! Quick boys, hose him down." Bruce shouted to the crew on the line.

When Billy took off his helmet and air mask, his eyes were

as big as saucers. "Bruce!" he shouted. "Do you realize what happened?"

"Yeah, Billy," Bruce smiled. "There was a flashover."

"No, not that. I thought I was dead! I saw this ball of fire coming right at me. When it hit me – BOOM! I thought I was dead. But I'm not dead. I'm here. I beat it. I beat the 'Red Devil!'"

"You sure did, kid," Bruce chuckled. "Come on, we'd better get you looked at."

"I'm fine, I want to go back inside!"

Bruce stared down at the young mans hands. "Actually, I think you need to go and get checked out." The smoldering gloves told him that Billy had serious burns.

As Billy followed Bruce's eyes, a searing pain ripped upward from his fingertips at the realization he'd been burned. He took a deep breath and refused to give in. "I'll just change my gloves," he winced. "I'll be fine."

"Don't argue with me," Bruce firmly stated. "You're going to the hospital and that's the end of it."

Billy hung his head in disappointment. "Yes, Sir."

"Now, get going. That's an order!"

"Yes, Sir." Billy took a step towards the ambulance then stopped and turned back to Bruce. "Is Wells okay?" He asked.

Bruce shook his head. "I don't know. The Captain's still inside looking for him."

The rookie's face turned white. "They haven't found him yet?"

"No. But they better find him soon."

Billy didn't like Michael Wells. The guy had a huge ego and he wasn't a team player. Michael thought he was God's gift to women and he hit on everything that moved. Lately, Billy had noticed Sarah acting strange whenever Michael was around. Maybe he'd hit on her, too.

No matter what Billy thought of Michael personally, at work, Michael was part of the brotherhood of the fire department, part of the family. You did everything you could to save family.

"Don't worry, kid," Bruce smiled. "We'll find them. Now

get going." He turned to walk away then stopped and glanced back over his shoulder. "Hey kid, you did a great job tonight."

"Thanks." Billy gave Bruce a proud smile. "Does that mean I get to take fire watch next tour?"

"You bet your boots it does kid," Bruce laughed.

Chapter Twenty

THE FIRE WAS SPECTACULAR. Flames shot into the night sky like a rocket on the fourth of July and the surrounding streets were lit up as if by the noonday sun. The fire department blocked off one full city block with yellow tape that acted like an invisible barrier wall to keep curious onlookers at bay. Police cars, parked nose to nose, their red and blue lights flashing, re-routed traffic at the four major intersections leading to the fire. Patrolmen guarded the perimeter and the area was sealed off tighter than Fort Knox. The only people allowed anywhere near the scene were firefighters, EMS, cops and reporters.

"May I see your press pass Miss," the officer asked.

Jane reached down the front of her black leather jacket and pulled out the chain that held her identification. "Here you go," she smiled.

"Thank you, Miss Phillips. The media tent is set up beside the command post. A block straight ahead."

She didn't normally come to these things. She usually got her information from Kurt, or one of the boys at KLCY, but she happened to be in the neighborhood, so she decided to check it out.

As she walked towards the action, the sound of sirens coming from every direction told her that this must be a big one. If they'd called a second alarm, soon there would be double the equipment and double the manpower. The engine and ladder trucks from Station's No. 21 and No. 16 would be on their way, as would the Battalion Chief, the emergency rescue unit, mobile command and the Public Information Officer.

When Jane reached the media tent, it was filled with reporters from every newspaper and TV station in the city. She grabbed a coffee and made her way over to where the camera crew of KLCY was setting up to do a live feed.

"This must be a biggie!" Jane remarked as she leaned over and gave TJ Rice a peck on the cheek.

"Hey, Jane." TJ smiled, "the boys have a wild one on their hands, that's for sure."

"Really? What's the scope?"

"Engine Company No. 5 was the first to arrive. Apparently, when they got here, two of the crew went inside to look for the owner's kid."

"The owner's kid?"

TJ shook his head. "Yeah, that's Brandon's Furniture Store going up like a Roman candle. Anyway, they found the kid, but lost a firefighter in the process. So the captain went in with his rookie to find the guy."

"Did you say Engine Company No. 5?" Jane asked.

"Yeah, Ben Taylor's crew." TJ gave her a puzzled look. "Hey, wait a minute, doesn't your boyfriend work at No. 5?"

"That's not important right now." Jane pulled out her notepad and flipped to a blank page. "Tell me what's going on with the fire?"

"They found the kid. One of the guys from No. 5 brought him out."

"Is the owner here?"

"No, not that I know of."

"How's the kid? Can he talk?"

"It looks like he's in pretty bad shape. The information we got, said he was unconscious when they brought him out of the building."

Jane gave a sigh of relief. She didn't want to interview Stan Brandon. Not here, and certainly not now. "Are there any firefighters hurt?" She asked.

TJ shook his head. "Well, I'd assume, the guy who went down. As far as I know, they haven't found him yet."

Chapter Twenty One

AT THE TOP OF THE stairs, Ben turned left and disappeared into the smoke. He knew he was going to have one hell of a time finding Michael, it was as black as a train tunnel.

He'd traveled ahead on his hands and knees no more than three feet when Bruce's voice broke in over the radio. "Captain, did you see the flashover?"

"No, but I heard it. Is everyone okay?" Ben asked.

"Negative," Bruce answered. "The kid got blown down the stairs."

"How badly is he hurt?"

"Burns to his neck and hands. I think it scared the shit out of him more than it hurt him," Bruce chuckled. "He wanted to go back inside. He's on his way to the hospital now. Have you found Wells?"

"Negative. I can't hear his pal going off and I can't see a bloody thing up here. Are you back inside?"

"Yeah, just coming up the stairs. Pete and Garth are right ahead of me. They'll grab the line I extended on the first go round and protect our avenue of escape. I'll follow your line and be there in a jiffy."

The next radio transmission the men heard was cause for concern. "Command. This is attack team one. We aren't gonna be able to stay in here much longer. The ceiling's rolling like a tidal wave and it's hotter than a firecracker. Look's like the fire's punched holes in the roof. It's starting to free vent. I think we need to go surround and drown on this baby, and soon!"

Ben knew if that were the case, any minute there would be

a recall. The warning horns would go off and everybody would be ordered out of the building. He'd have to abandon his search.

He was sure the incoming ladders had already set up water curtains to protect the exposures and save the buildings on either side. 17's attack team sounded like they had a few minutes. Pete and Garth were on their way up, they'd be grabbing water. Bruce had once lifted the back end of a one-ton pick-up truck off a child to save its life. *I'm in good hands.* Ben told himself.

As quickly as he could, he moved blindly through the smoke. He stopped when he heard the faint squealing sound and reached for his mike button. "I think I can hear Wells' personal alarm system going off. It sounds like it's somewhere in front of me. I'm going forward."

Ben crawled ahead on his hands and knees, searching for obstacles in his path. The high pitched squeal was getting louder and he knew he must be close. He reached sideways, and his gloved hand was stopped by something solid. He felt the object – it was a boot. He moved his hand up Michael's leg. At his knees, he found the bookcase. He hit the button on his radio. "Command, I've found Wells, but I can't get him out by myself. He's trapped under something."

Chapter Twenty Two

JANE SPENT FIVE MINUTES looking for Mark Turner, but he was nowhere to be found. She was about to head out of the tent when TJ stopped her.

"Hey, Jane. We've got a problem."

"What's up?"

"Candice just called from her cell phone. She's stuck in traffic. We need to go live in five. Can you help out?"

Jane shook her head and laughed. "Me? You want me to do your live feed for you? You've got to be out of your mind TJ, I'm a reporter, not a newscaster."

He looked at her with big puppy dog eyes. "Oh, come on," he begged. "It's not like you haven't done this before. You used to do live shoots when you worked in Denver."

As the words came out of TJ's mouth, every muscle in Jane's body tightened. "How do you know about that?"

"Kurt told me."

"Kurt told you?"

"Yeah, last week when I ran into him at the Hose and Hydrant. So, listen, are you going to do this thing for me or not?"

Jane was fuming. How the hell did Kurt find out that she worked in Denver? She didn't even have the same last name for Christ's sake. This had to be stopped. She had to shut the little weasel up before he ruined everything.

"Jane." TJ gave her a nudge. "Are you going to do this thing for me or not?"

"I don't think so," she coldly replied.

As Jane turned to walk away, TJ grabbed her by the arm.

"Come on, will you please help me out? I've done you a favor or two before. Besides, you're always looking for free publicity and positive press. Maybe you'll gain some new fans." He offered her his best smile. "What do you say?"

For a moment, Jane thought about the picture Kurt had faxed to her. It was a clear indication of what the fire department thought of her. That kind of press she didn't need. Her father always told her that you caught more flies with honey than vinegar. Maybe it was time to change the department's mind.

"Let's move it people," someone yelled. "We're on in four."

"Alright, TJ. I'll do this, but you owe me."

He gave her a peck on the cheek. "No, sweetheart, it's you, who'll owe me. After this, you'll be famous."

That's what she was afraid of.

Chapter Twenty Three

THIRTY-YEAR OLD FIRE arson investigator, Lieutenant Heather Kennedy sat in silent reflection as she stared down at the bandaged face and arms of firefighter Michael Wells. *How ironic*, she thought. The last time she'd been in a hospital room, she was the one lying in bed wrapped in flamazine dressings.

Heather put her left hand inside her shirt and felt the beginning of the scar that ran from her right shoulder, across her chest, and down the middle of her stomach to her waist. The physical pain of her injury had long since vanished, but mentally, she knew she still had issues to deal with. For a brief moment, she felt sorry for herself. Then she remembered that her classmate and good friend, Travis Greenwood, died that night in Chicago.

To this day, she still couldn't believe that the smoke detectors in Travis's apartment hadn't gone off. The batteries were dead. Travis was a firefighter for God sake. He'd never overlook something like that. Heather found the whole thing unsettling.

The last time Heather was in Chicago, she paid a visit to Fire Department Headquarters and looked at Travis' arson file. As always, Bart Campbell had done a systematic investigation. He'd walked through the fire scene looking for the obvious. He'd taken picture after picture of the burned apartment.

In the living room, he discovered a melted plastic ashtray. In the carpet, he found evidence of alcohol. His tests indicated it was Jack Daniel's. Heather knew that Travis didn't smoke and the only time he drank Jack was when he was fishing with the boys. Someone else had to have been there.

In the bedroom, all clues to the cause of the blaze lead to an electrical outlet beside Travis' bed, but it didn't make sense to her that an outlet could short circuit when there was nothing plugged into it.

The police investigation told her that Travis didn't have any skeletons hiding in his closet. He wasn't into a local loan shark for copious amounts of cash and he didn't have any crazed ex-girlfriends.

The autopsy report indicated that Travis had been drugged. It blew her away to think that someone may have tried to kill him, but who and why she had no idea.

"Hi, how's Michael doing?"

The sound of a male voice brought Heather back to the present. She turned in her chair and gave Ben Taylor a warm smile. "He hasn't moved in the last hour."

"He shouldn't be here," Ben remarked as he walked to the bed. "He knows better than to split up the team."

"Yeah, I know," Heather nodded in agreement.

Ben gave her a tired smile. "Listen, I'm gonna head back to the hall. Are you going to be here for awhile?"

"I was just about to go down and see how the Brandon kid is doing. I really need to talk to him. There's something about this fire that isn't right. The second floor of the building looks like it may have been booby trapped."

"Yeah, Bruce mentioned something about that. He said there was a piece of wire strung across the floor where he found the kid."

Heather shook her head. "That was the first suspicious thing that hit me. The major part of the fire took place in the front corner of the store, but I'm positive that's not where it started. As far as the Brandon kid is concerned. I don't think he was the target. I think he just happened to be in the wrong place at the wrong time."

"What makes you say that?" Ben asked.

"Well, I read about a similar fire in Detroit where the arsonist set traps. It was in the garage of a trucking company. The fire bug propped tractor-trailer tires up on two-by-fours."

"The guy must have been strong, those things aren't light."

"Anyway, before he left the scene, he wrapped the base of each two-by-four with gasoline soaked rags. It was a good trap, it killed a firefighter."

"Did they ever catch the guy?" Ben asked.

"No. There was a lot of overwhelming evidence that the fire had been deliberately set, but they never found a suspect. They went through the owner's business records with a fine tooth comb, and they couldn't find any insurance issues. When they did a personal background check, he came out smelling like a rose. His employees all loved him and he didn't have any enemies." Heather turned her attention back to Michael. "No Ben, I'm sure that whoever did this was after a firefighter. The only reason the kid got hurt was because he happened to be in the wrong place at the wrong time. Hopefully, he can tell us who his last customer was."

"Well, I don't think the kid will be able to tell you much of anything," Ben frowned. "He hasn't regained consciousness, and when he does, the doctor says it's going to be awhile before he'll be able to speak. His windpipe was badly burned." Ben ran his hands through his hair and let out an exhausted sigh. "You know, by all accounts, the Brandon kid should be dead. He's very lucky to be alive."

"Someone was watching out for him," Heather smiled. "Well, I might as well go back to headquarters." She stood up and pulled her daytimer from her pocket. "Have you got anything planned for the crew tomorrow night?"

"We were going out on inspections, but I'd imagine you want to have a chat with the boys?"

Heather nodded her head. "Have the coffee on. I'll be there at eight."

"Okay," Ben winked. "I'll see you tomorrow."

As he turned to leave, Heather called after him. "I forgot to ask. How's your rookie?"

"He'll be okay. They had to cut the gloves off his hands and the doctors say he may need a skin graft, but other than that, he'll be fine." Ben gave her a proud grin. "Billy's got guts, I'll give him that. Bruce had to fight with the kid to get him in the bus. He wanted to go back inside."

Heather let out a chuckle as she headed towards the door. "Rookies, what can I say? Is anyone with him?"

"His fiancé, Sarah. Nice girl, I don't think you've met her. She said she'd drive him home when the doctors were finished with him."

"I just heard about Michael," Jane Phillips announced as she barged into the hospital room. "Is he going to be okay?"

She pushed her way past Heather and Ben and hurried to the bed. "Oh, my God. Look at you, Michael. You're not dead! I can't believe it, you're not dead!" She turned to Heather and Ben. "May we have a few minutes alone, please?"

Chapter Twenty Four

RACHEL MCCAULEY PRESSED THE doorbell of Fire Hall No. 5 and as she waited nervously for someone to answer, she read the poem on the bronze plaque attached to the building. It was titled 'The Firefighters Prayer'.

*When I am called to duty God
Whenever flames may rage
Give me strength to save some life
Whatever be its age*

*Help me embrace a little child
Before it is to ...*

At the sound of the deadbolt, Rachel turned her attention from the poem, and watched as a gray haired gentleman opened the door.

"Hi. What can I help you with today?" he asked.

"Hello," she blushed. "Would Captain Taylor be here by any chance?"

"You bet. Come on in." Bruce led Rachel into the alarm room and picked up the speakerphone. "Captain Taylor to the alarm room. You have a visitor." He motioned to the chair beside the desk. "Have a seat. He should be with you in a jiffy."

"Thank you." Rachel offered him a polite smile and glided across the room. "There must be something special going on today, you're wearing your No. 1 dress uniform."

Bruce's smile faded instantly. "We're just on our way to a funeral."

"Oh, I'm so sorry," she apologized. "I had no idea."

He offered her a forgiving grin. "It's okay. You wouldn't have known. We lost one of our crew members a few days ago."

"I read in the paper that a firefighter had died, but I had no idea he was from this hall. Maybe I should come back another time."

"No, no, it's okay. The Captain will be here in a flash. He's just finishing up with the new rookie." Bruce checked his watch. "We still have a few minutes before we have to leave and unless you're trying to sell him life insurance, I'm sure he'll have a minute or two for a beautiful young lady such as yourself."

"Why, thank you," she blushed.

"Make yourself comfortable. He won't be long."

While Rachel waited for Ben's arrival, she scanned the memos and maps tacked to the wall. "I wonder what would happen if I pushed this?" She asked out loud as she ran her fingers over the switches of the alarm board.

"I wouldn't touch that if I were you," Ben commented from the doorway. "You'll be interrupting the boys lunch." He watched with interest as the dark haired woman spun around in her chair. Her face was red with embarrassment. "Hello." Ben extended his hand. "I'm Captain Taylor. What can I do for you this afternoon?"

The attractive brunette gave him a curious smile as she stood up. "You don't remember me, do you Ben?" She asked as he walked towards her.

He thought for a moment. The face was familiar, and there was something about the voice, but he just couldn't put his finger on it. "I'm sorry to say, that I don't. Did we meet at one of the fire department charity fundraisers?"

"It's me, Ben. Rachel McCauley."

Suddenly, her face was as familiar to him as if he'd seen it only yesterday. "Rachel McCauley. I don't believe it. I haven't seen you in years."

"Hello, Ben." She offered him her hand.

"Oh, come here. We've known each other too long for just a hand shake." He pulled her into his arms and gave her a warm hug. "What are you doing here? How did you find me?"

"Actually," she blushed, "I read in the paper a few weeks ago that you were getting an award at the Firefighters' gala, and I was going to go, hoping that I'd catch up to you. Then, this morning, I got a phone call saying that the event was being postponed until October. So, I called headquarters and told them I was your sister. They gave me the address of the hall and told me you'd be here."

This time, Ben's face turned red. "I'm flattered. You seem to have gone to a lot of trouble to find me."

Rachel took a deep breath and smiled back at him. "Well, I'm fairly new to the city. I don't know very many people and I was hoping that perhaps, we could re-kindle an old friendship. I can see that now isn't a good time. Your nozzle man told me that you were just leaving for a funeral."

Ben shook his head and motioned for her to sit down. "Yeah, Michael Wells, one of my crew members. He'd only been stationed here for six months."

"I read about Michael's death in the paper, but I had no idea he was from this hall."

Ben perched himself on the corner of the desk. "I still can't believe we lost him."

"What happened?" Rachel quietly asked.

"It was that furniture store fire two weeks ago. I'm sure you read about it in the paper."

She nodded her head. "Yes, yes I did."

"Michael got trapped under a bookcase."

"Oh, my God, that's awful."

"He was in pretty bad shape when we finally got him out of the fire, badly broken and burned, but he was still breathing. We thought he'd be okay. The doctors said, other than some scarring on his chest and arms and his broken bones mending, he was expected to make a full recovery."

"Did something go wrong?" She asked.

Ben shrugged his shoulders. "I'm not sure. I don't have all

the details, but from what I understand, he died of complications. It just doesn't make any sense."

Rachel shifted nervously in her chair. "It must be a very difficult time for all of you."

"Excuse me, Captain," Bruce interrupted. "The boys are about ready to leave with the engine."

"Thanks, Bruce," Ben smiled. "I'll be there in a minute."

Rachel quickly got up from the chair. "Listen Ben, I really think that maybe I should just leave you my number. You can give me a call at a more convenient time."

He reached out and took her hand "You know something, now is a good time. I hate funerals and this is the second one I've been to in three months."

"It wasn't another firefighter was it?" She asked.

"Yeah, a senior man from 'C' shift."

"I hope he died of natural causes."

Ben shook his head. "No, he didn't. He was inside knocking down the blaze and he fell through a hole in the floor."

Rachel looked at Ben with a sad smile. "I don't understand how any of you can do this job. How do you deal with the tragedy you see everyday?"

"Some guys never do," Ben replied. "They never get over losing a crew mate, but the department offers counseling..."

"Ben, I'm sorry to keep bugging you, but we really need to get going."

"Okay, Bruce. I'll be right there." He looked back at Rachel. She was still as beautiful and as kind as he remembered her being and he decided to go out on a limb. "If you're not doing anything for the next couple of hours, and you want to be a friend, how about coming with me. I could really use your support. I'll introduce you as my sister."

Rachel let out a chuckle and shook her head. "Oh, I don't think so Ben. Why don't I give you a call next week?"

"I'd really like you to come Rachel. We have to go to the funeral home first and pick up the casket, but ..."

Shocked erupted on her face. "What do you mean, you have to pick up the casket? Doesn't the funeral home usually do that?"

"Not for our funerals. Not when a firefighter is killed in the line of duty. When that happens, it's customary to carry his casket from the funeral home, to the church, on top of the engine from the fire hall he was stationed at. Michael was stationed here, at No. 5, so his body will ride on the hose bed of our engine and we'll put his helmet inside the rig on the seat he always occupied."

Rachel shook her head in confusion. "The hose bed?"

"Oh, sorry," Ben apologized. "I guess you don't understand fire department lingo. The top of our fire engine is called the hose bed. It's where we keep the hose, of course."

He turned her around and pointed towards the apparatus floor. His body gave a shiver when his hand touched her shoulder. "See, up there. I'll be riding in there with my crew, but you can follow us in your car. Once we get to the funeral home, just file into the procession and I'll meet you at the church. It's only a few blocks away."

Chapter Twenty Five

"MICHAEL'S FUNERAL WAS VERY nice," Rachel quietly remarked in Ben's direction. "I can't get over the number of people. I'm sure the church was packed to capacity. I felt so sorry for his mother, the poor woman. That eulogy was so emotional. I don't think there was a dry eye in the place. It was such a nice touch when the Fire Department Chaplain, Reverend Douglas, read the Firefighter's Prayer afterwards. His soothing voice had a way of calming everyone.

"Did you see that one guy during communion? He grabbed the goblet out of the Reverend's hand and poured back the wine like he was doing a shooter!"

As Rachel heard the words coming out of her mouth, she stopped in mid sentence. *You're making an idiot out of yourself. You sound like an inconsiderate sixteen-year-old. Shut up for God sake. Quit while you're still ahead*, she firmly told herself. She turned to Ben and apologized. "Oh, Ben, I'm sorry. I've been rambling on and on, and not even taking your feelings into consideration." She paused for a moment before adding, "I guess it's nerves."

"What's there to be nervous about?" He reached across the seat and gave her hand an affectionate squeeze. "I don't bite."

"It's not you," she blushed. "It's just, that, well, it's been a long time since I've been to a funeral. The last time was my uncle's."

Rachel pulled a Kleenex from her handbag and dabbed at the tear forming in the corner of her eye. "He died in a fire," she sniffed. "So did one of the firefighters who tried to save him. The firefighter's wife was a very close friend of my aunt's. I went to both men's funerals. It was terrible. My aunt and the firefighter's wife were devastated. It broke my heart and I swore then and there that I'd never get married. I couldn't stand losing someone I loved that much."

Ben squeezed her hand a little tighter. "Oh, Rachel, I'm so sorry. I had no idea. When did it happen?"

"I'd really rather not talk about it if you don't mind," Rachel answered in a whisper.

"But, if you ever do want to talk about it, I'm here to listen. We counsel a lot of people on fire deaths and how to cope with them."

"Thank you Ben, I appreciate it." She turned to him and smiled. "If I ever need to talk, I'll let you know."

"Well, I really appreciate you coming with me today. I'm not a big fan of funerals either."

"Ben, do you think we could change the subject?" Rachel asked.

"Good idea. Listen, I know that I've asked a lot of you today, but I have one more favor."

"What's that?"

"Are you doing anything right now? Do you have to be anywhere?"

"Why?"

"Well, I was talking to some of the guys at the cemetery, and we're all going to meet for a drink. I'd like you to come along."

Rachel checked her watch. It was 4:30. "Well, okay, I don't have any pressing matters on my desk, and I'm not meeting clients until later, so yes, I'd love to go with you!"

Chapter Twenty Six

THE HOSE AND HYDRANT was packed to capacity with uniformed firefighters all tipping a glass to Michael Wells. "There's the guys." Ben pointed to a table in the corner. "Come on." He took Rachel by the hand and led her through the crowd.

"Nice of you to show up Captain," Bruce belched from behind his beer mug. "You're about three pitchers behind us," he announced.

"Unfortunately, it's going to have to stay that way," Ben chuckled. "I'm on a diet."

"Yeah, you should diet! You probably haven't seen it for years," Tom Chambers, Ben's best friend yelled from the end of the table.

Bruce gave Rachel a drunken smile. "Come on little lady." He pushed his chair back, and patted his hands on his lap. "Have a seat. We'll take care of you. The fat old fart can go sit somewhere else."

Rachel turned to Ben, her eyes were as big as saucers. "What should I do?" she mouthed.

Ben leaned over and whispered in her ear. "It's okay, Bruce's bark is a lot worse than his bite. He's had a few, but you don't have to worry about him groping you or anything. He's a big teddy bear. Our Christmas Santa Claus in fact."

Ben took her by the arm and moved towards the table. "Rachel McCauley, I'd like you to meet my crew, and their significant others," he proudly announced. "You've met Bruce. This is his wife, Alice."

The women exchanged a nod.

Ben motioned to the next couple. "Lieutenant Pete Metcalfe and his wife, Carol."

Pete stood up and offered Rachel his hand. "Actually, we've met."

"You have?" Ben remarked in surprise.

"Yeah," Pete smiled, "when we were doing house to house inspections. Don't you remember?"

Rachel's face turned red with embarrassment. She knew what the rumor mill was like at the fire department. She could only hope that Pete hadn't gotten wind of her little date with Michael. It was obvious to this point that Ben didn't know anything about it. She gave Pete a broad smile. "Yes, yes I do. It's nice to see you again."

"I didn't know that you lived in our district," Ben grinned.

"Yes. I have a place in the Bluffs."

"Pretty ritzy area," Tony piped up. "Hi, I'm Tony DeMonte." He stuck out his hand. "Nice to meet you Rachel. So, you live in the Bluffs do you? I hate fighting fires up there. Those places are like a maze with rounded walls and spiral staircases. A man-made death trap. It's a bitch I tell yeah."

He gave the attractive woman a boyish grin and eyed her from top to bottom. She was well turned out. "Well Rachel," he grinned, "you must be independently wealthy, or have a really good job, those places are damn expensive."

"Real estate has been very good to me," she blushed. She was wealthy, monetarily. Now, after running into Ben again after all these years, perhaps her emotional needs would be met too.

Pete gave Tony a friendly shove. "Sit down Tony, and quit trying to pick up the Captain's girlfriend." He turned his attention back to the beauty in front of him. "Rachel, this is my wife, Carol."

"Nice to meet you, Carol," Rachel smiled.

"You too," Carol smiled back.

Ben pointed down the table. "That guy at the end of the table, the one whose wife put me on this diet, is my best friend, Captain Tom Chambers. The breath of fresh air sitting beside him is his charming wife, Katherine. How she's put up with him for all these years is beyond my imagination." Ben leaned over and whispered in Rachel's ear. "Six months from now, they'll be jetting off to Maui to celebrate their twenty-fifth wedding anniversary."

"That's fantastic. Most marriages don't last that long."

"Beside Tom and Katherine," Ben continued, "is our rookie, Billy Simpson, and his fiancé, Sarah Baker."

Rachel waved in their direction. "Nice to meet both of you."

Sarah and Billy nodded in reply.

"Last, but not least, "Garth Hanson and his wife, Barb."

When Rachel and Ben sat down, Billy leaned over and whispered in Sarah's ear. "Do you remember me telling you that Michael picked up a woman one day when we were out doing inspections? He was going to take her to the gala."

"Yes," Sarah replied.

"Well, that's her."

She turned to Billy in surprise. "What do you mean that's her?"

"That's her. That's the dame he was going to take to the gala.

"You're kidding me, right?"

"No, I'm not kidding. That's her!"

"But, I thought Michael was going out with Jane Phillips?"

"I hate to speak ill of the dead," Billy whispered, "but Michael Wells hit on anything that moved." He leaned back and gave his bride-to-be a concerned look. "Did he ever hit on you?"

Sarah quickly shook her head. "No, no, Michael never hit on me. Let's talk about something else." She turned her attention back to Rachel. "What is she doing here with Ben?" Sarah asked.

Billy gave her a puzzled look. "She was at Michael's funeral with him, didn't you see her?"

"I couldn't see anything. Jane Phillips was sitting in front of me."

"Yeah, so?"

"Didn't you see that ghastly hat she was wearing? It was huge! A fashion don't!" Sarah looked back in Rachel and Ben's direction. "Anyway, back to my question, what's that woman doing here with Ben?"

"I have no idea," Billy answered, "but you can be sure that Pete's wife will find out. She could get a confession out of a dead man," he laughed. "You should really talk to Carol. She's the vice-president of Helping Hands, the fire department's ladies association. It would be good for you to get out and meet some of the other guy's wives."

Billy hoped that this time Sarah would take his suggestion. He'd been bugging her for months about getting involved with the fire department's ladies group. He figured it would do her a world of good. She'd been acting strange for weeks, but more so since Michael's death. Maybe she was having second thoughts about the wedding and marrying a firefighter. He'd talk to her when they got home.

In the background, Sarah could hear Billy's voice but she paid it little attention. She was too busy examining the woman on Ben's arm. She could see why Michael had asked her out. She was very attractive. In fact, she looked a little like Janis had looked in her prime. She had long dark hair, big blue eyes and a pearly white smile.

"She looks pleasant enough," Sarah remarked in Billy's direction.

"Did you say something?" Billy asked.

"Yes. I said she looks pleasant enough."

"Oh yeah, Carol's great."

"Not Carol." She gave him a punch in the arm. "The brunette, with Ben."

"Oh, the brunette. Yeah, she's nice too. You should see her house Sarah, it's a mansion!" He put his arm around her shoulder. "Someday we're going to have a place just like it."

"I don't think the Chief's job pays that much. Does it?" She leaned over and gave him a peck on the cheek. "I don't need a mansion. All I need is you to take care of me. You will do that won't you, Billy?"

"Of course, I'll take care of you Sarah. I'll take care of you forever. Nothing will ever hurt you as long as I'm around."

"Do you love me?" she asked.

"Now what kind of a question is that? Of course I love you. Would I have asked you to marry me if I didn't love you?"

"And you'll stand behind me, and support me, no matter what happens?"

"Yeah, that's what a husband does for a wife." He pulled her closer and whispered in her ear, "I'll always take care of you, Sarah."

At the other end of the table, Bruce stood up, excused himself and walked to the center of the room. "Ladies and gentleman," he began. "Can we have a little quiet here, please." A waitress rang the brass fire bell at the end of the bar and the room fell silent.

"Now that we're all here, I would like to say something." His body swayed from side to side as he raised his beer mug into the air. "First of all, I hope everyone can forgive me for my drunken stupor, but there are guys here who know exactly what I'm going through. What we're all going through."

He looked around the room. "Kip, you know what I'm talking about. Three months ago you lost one of your guys. You too Elliot. We all know it wasn't our fault, but the guilt eats away inside of us like acid on paint." Bruce raised his glass a little higher. "Michael, I gotta tell yah. I didn't' always like you, in fact there were times when you really pissed me off, but you were one of my brothers man, and I should have saved your ass. I'm sorry buddy, I'm really sorry."

Bruce took a deep breath and stood up tall. "You always fashioned yourself somewhat of a ladies man Michael. I can only hope that heaven has lots of chicks to admire the uniform you so proudly wore."

"Here, here," the group toasted.

Uniform he proudly wore my ass, Sarah thought to herself as she picked up her wineglass.

When quiet returned to the crowd, Bruce continued. "Now, I'd like to make another toast. A toast to the bastard who's torching buildings all over town, and killing us off, like flies. It's one thing to set the place on fire, but to set traps to get us while we're inside doing our job is something totally different. If this fire bug wanted to grab the department by the balls, he's succeeded."

Bruce's wife, Alice, stood up from the table. "Here we go again," she remarked to Ben and Rachel. "Will you two excuse me. I'd better get him off this soap box."

Rachel leaned closer to Ben. "What's Bruce talking about?"

"Oh, our last couple of fires."

"What about them?"

"The buildings were booby-trapped."

Rachel shook her head. "What do you mean they were booby-trapped?"

"Whoever is setting these fires, has also been setting traps inside the building."

"I don't understand?"

"Well, take Michael's fire for example. When Heather Kennedy from arson went inside to investigate, she found trip wires."

"So, what you're telling me is that someone is deliberately out to get firefighters."

"It seems that way."

PART TWO

Chapter Twenty Seven

THE GRANDFATHER CLOCK IN the front foyer of 397 Seaport Drive struck nine as Katherine Chambers walked through the front door. *I should have been home hours ago*, she reminded herself. She still had some last minute packing to do, but the girls wanted to take her out for dinner and she couldn't refuse. The evening lasted longer than Katherine expected.

She dropped her keys on the hall table and walked around the corner to hang up her leather jacket. It had been a hectic day and she was glad it was over. Preparations for the firefighters' gala were finally in place, again. Now she could relax and enjoy her second honeymoon.

When the event was postponed in June, due to the death of Michael Wells, the girls had to start from scratch. *Thank God for Rachel*, Katherine reminded herself. The woman had been a godsend during the past months. The fire department's ladies association would have been lost without her.

Katherine liked Rachel, she was good people and she could only hope that Ben would finally see the light and ask the girl to marry him. Christmas was coming up, maybe the festive mood would make him pop the question.

For the past fifteen years, Ben Taylor had shared Christmas and every other major holiday with the Chambers family. He was more like a brother to Tom and Katherine than a friend. More than once, Ben had filled in when Tom couldn't make it to his son's baseball game or his daughter's dance recital.

When Katherine's father was tragically killed in an automobile accident in Europe, it was Ben who escorted her to claim the body. When Tom was hurt on the job and Katherine held a vigil at the hospital, it was Ben who cared for the children.

Katherine felt secure in the knowledge that Ben had always watched Tom's back, although that had been easier when the two men worked on the same shift. Now, she took comfort that as a Captain, Tom rarely entered a burning building. When he first joined the department, she spent many sleepless nights worrying about him. She stopped worrying the day he was promoted.

Katherine let out an exhausted sigh and forced her weary legs to carry her down the hall to the kitchen. She was beat and all she wanted was a hot bath and a good night sleep. As she walked past the built-in oak desk on her way to the refrigerator, she noticed the message indicator light blinking. She pushed the button on the answering machine. "You have three messages," the familiar computerized voice announced.

"Hi Tom. Garry Newton, here. Just a reminder that if you're in on the ice fishing trip, registration is the end of the month. Give me a call." Katherine saved the message for Tom and went on to the next.

"Hi, Katie. It's Ben. I'm on my way to the hall, so Tom should be home soon. I had something really important to do. I'll tell you all about it when I pick you up for the airport in the morning. Have a good night."

The final message was from Rachel. " Hi, Kate. I won't bother calling you again, I'm sure you have a million things to do before you leave, but don't worry. The girls and I will take care of the last minute stuff for the gala so you just go and have fun. Enjoy your second honeymoon."

Katherine smiled as she erased the message. "I'm not going to worry Rachel. I'm going to go to Maui with my handsome husband and forget about the world."

She hung up the telephone, unloaded the dishwasher, went through the mail, and folded the laundry on the dryer. "There, that takes care of that." She poured herself a glass of wine and was just about to head upstairs and finish packing when the phone rang. "Hello," Katherine politely answered.

"Hi, sweetheart. It's me."

Her face lit up at the sound of Tom's voice. "Hi, are you on your way home? I was just going upstairs to start a tub."

"No," Tom replied. "Ben isn't here yet. I expected him half an hour ago."

"I just erased a message from him earlier. Let me check the time." Katherine looked down at the numbers on the phone. "Half an hour ago. The message said he was just leaving for the hall."

"Well, he isn't here yet. He must be caught in traffic."

"So, are we all set on the morning routine," Katherine asked.

"Yeah," Tom chuckled, "but you better run it by me again. You know what happens to a guy when he gets old."

She pulled her checklist from the desk drawer. "Well, Ben will be here as soon as he's off shift. Our first stop is Starbucks, of course."

Tom couldn't help but chuckle. Katie certainly loved her coffee. "You know dear, if you had all the money you've spent at Starbucks over the years, you could buy yourself one of those fancy coffee making machines and open your own Starbucks."

"Yes, that's true," Katherine agreed, "but it's been my experience, that no one makes a Breve Latte like Starbucks, including me. I tried the last time I was at Rachel's and it just couldn't compare to one made by a trained professional. Besides, Chris, and his staff are very good to me. I don't even have to order my drink. The minute they see me coming they start making it. By the time I'm finished at the register, it's waiting for me on the bar. Now that's what I call customer service!"

"You should head up their marketing department," Tom laughed.

"Never you mind," Katherine scolded. "Our next stop is the kennel to drop of Snider."

"What about the paper and the mail?" Tom asked.

"Sarah will be over every day to collect the mail and pick up ..."

"Hey, I just saw Ben's truck pull up," Tom interrupted. "I'll be home in a jiffy."

"Still interested in a tub?" Katherine asked. "Or are you too tired?"

"I'm never too tired for a tub with you," Tom chuckled. "I'll meet you in the pool!"

Chapter Twenty Eight

IT WAS 21:35 WHEN Ben pulled into the parking lot of Fire Hall No. 19, to cover the rest of Tom's shift. "Shit, I'm late. Katherine's going to kill me."

He'd promised her he'd be at the hall by nine and Tom would be home by now. *Not to worry,* he told himself. *Once she finds out why I was late, she'll forgive me.*

Ben shut off the truck and pulled down the sun visor. "Well, you've gone and done it now Taylor," he smiled at his reflection. "Soon, you'll be an old married man just like your buddy, Tom."

He'd done it all right! He'd asked Rachel McCauley to marry him and, other than leaving his father's company to join the fire department, Ben was confident it was the best decision he had ever made.

His friends all liked Rachel and according to Katherine, she was the best thing that had ever happened to him. "Ben, I have to be honest with you. This one's a keeper." Katherine had told him. "Since Tom and I have known you, you've dated some real winners, but Rachel, she's just great! She's not at all like Jane Phillips. I still can't believe you went out with that woman. Wasn't she what you guys call 'high maintenance? As far as her sense of humor went, well thank God, you discovered she didn't have one before you got serious about her."

As Katherine's words filled Ben's head, he couldn't help but laugh out loud remembering the incident she'd been referring to.

***

It was eleven months ago, in October. Ben and Jane had been invited to Tom and Katherine's lake front cottage in Northern Ontario to celebrate Canadian Thanksgiving. Like initiation of any new rookie into the fire hall, Tom's first order of business, was testing a new guest's sense of humor. His little practical joke had become somewhat of a tradition over the years and more than one victim, had fallen prey. Jane Phillips fell the hardest.

While Katherine was entertaining Jane, and a few of the neighbors down at the lake, Tom and Ben slipped away and snuck up the hill to the garage. Tom grabbed a fishing pole off the wall and a spool of fishing line from his tackle box. "Here," he handed Ben two fishing hooks. "Put these in your pocket and grab the step ladder."

With devious grins, the two over-grown children left the garage and headed to the house to initiate the first part of Tom's three-part, guaranteed to scare the stuffing out of you, gag.

"Do we need cup hooks?" Ben asked as they walked into the kitchen.

"No. I've already got hooks fastened into the ceiling upstairs. This isn't the first time I've done this you know."

"How long have you been pulling this little practical joke of yours?"

"Well, let's see." Tom reached up and scratched his whiskered chin. "Katherine and I will be married twenty-four years this year. Her father pulled this gag on me the first Christmas I every stayed at his place. That was twenty-three years ago, so it's been awhile."

"It's a good one. I'll give you that," Ben laughed.

"Yeah, it sure is. I've decided to take it on the road. I'm going to pull it on my next new rookie. You ready?" Tom asked

"Good to go!"

As the two men rounded the top of the stairs, Tom stopped in his tracks and turned to Ben. "Maybe we should wait till later to do this. It's kind of chilly out tonight. What happens if Jane comes up to get a sweater?"

"Are you kidding," Ben laughed. "If she puts on a sweater, no one will be able to see, or admire, that diamond pendant she's got hanging around her neck."

"Yeah, I noticed." Tom raised a questioning brow. "Did you give it to her?"

"No," Ben chuckled. "Actually, tonight is the first time I've seen it myself. She told me it was a gift from her father."

"That's quite a rock. Her old man must have bucks" Tom remarked as they entered the spare bedroom. "So, you realize of course, if you hook up with her permanently, you better be prepared to keep her in the life style she seems to be accustomed to."

"I don't think this one's a keeper, Tom. Sometimes I think the only reason she's going out with me is to pump me for information."

"What do you mean?"

"She appears to have a real interest in arson."

"So why did you bring her up here this weekend?"

"Well," Ben grinned, "the way I see it, if she's got a sense of humor then she can't be all bad. Right?"

Tom checked his watch. "Well, my friend, in about two hours, we're going to find out just how much of a sense of humor she's got. Have you got the fishing hooks?" He asked.

"Right here," Ben reached into the pocket of his denim jacket and pulled out the shiny metal objects.

"Okay, thread the line through both hooks," Tom told him.

"Done," Ben smiled. "Where do you want me to put them?"

Tom looked down from the ladder and pointed towards the bright patchwork quilt covering the bed. "It's been my experience that this works best if you stick the hooks side by side in the bottom right corner of the quilt."

Ben followed his instructions. "What's next?"

"Hand me up the fishing line. I'll run it through the cup hooks, across the ceiling, and out the bedroom door. From there, it runs down the hallway and into the den." Tom positioned the fishing line. "Yup, Miss Jane Phillips is in for one hell of a surprise tonight when she crawls into bed and I start reeling in the catch of the day!" Tom looked over his shoulder and smiled at Ben. "You realize you may be in the doghouse after this."

"It's a chance I'm willing to take," Ben smiled back.

When the boys returned to the beach, Tom gave Katherine a kiss on the cheek. It was a signal that everything was in place.

"Where have you been Ben?" Jane asked. There was a tone of annoyance in her voice. "You've been gone for over half an hour."

"Oh, sorry," he apologized. Tom and I just had some stuff to take care of for the volunteer fire department Christmas fundraiser."

"Come here," she demanded. "I'm freezing." Jane motioned to the vacant seat beside her and Ben sat down.

"Would you like me to go up to the house and get you a sweater?" He asked.

She smiled politely, reached up to the gold chain hanging from her neck and rolled the diamond in her fingers. "No, it's okay," she smiled. "You can keep me warm." She put her arm around him and pulled him closer.

"Has everyone got a hot chocolate?" Tom asked. "If so, then I guess it's time."

"Time for what?" Jane asked.

"Time to toast our local ghost," Katherine told her.

"Excuse me, your local ghost? What ghost?" Jane's eyes darted back and forth between Tom and Katherine. "What are you talking about?"

"You're not afraid of ghosts are you Jane?" Tom asked.

"No, I'm not afraid of ghosts. In fact, I don't believe in ghosts."

Tom shook his head. "Well, maybe you wouldn't be so skeptical if you'd seen her."

"And I suppose you have?"

"Oh, yes, more than once," Katherine smiled.

Tom sat down beside his wife, leaned forward and rested his hands on his knees. "Would you like me to tell you about our ghost?"

Jane raised a sarcastic brow. "I don't believe in ghosts, Tom, but if it will make you happy, by all means, be my guest." She folded her arms across her chest and leaned back in her chair.

"Twenty years ago," Tom began, "a newlywed couple took a room at the lodge across the lake to celebrate their first wedding anniversary. Unbeknownst to the bride, her much older husband was only after one thing. He wanted her money. He'd been planning her demise since before the wedding and the weekend excursion was only a ploy to get rid of her once and for all.

"As the story goes, he decided to take her somewhere where he could murder her, bury the body, and no one would be any the wiser. What better place than the lodge." Tom pointed to the lights across lake.

"That night, they shared a romantic candlelight dinner and afterwards he suggested the two of them take a moonlit stroll. When she agreed, he took her off the beaten path claiming that he'd found the perfect spot where the water was so still, looking in it was like looking in a mirror. It was the perfect place for an intimate romantic interlude. He'd been there earlier and everything was arranged.

"When they reached the place he'd spoken of, he took her hand and encouraged her to kneel beside the waters edge. He smiled down at her reflection and told her that he always wanted to remember how beautiful she looked in the moonlight.

"He gave her a kiss and put his large hand on the back of her head. 'If you look real close', he told her, 'you'll be able to see the reflection of the moon in your eyes'.

"Trusting her husband with her life, the young woman offered no resistance as his hand gently pushed her head forward. When her beautiful, innocent face was no more than six inches from the icy water, he pushed her head under, and held it there with his powerful hands until she stopped fighting him."

Tom cleared his throat. "Assuming his wife was dead, the man dragged her limp body into the bushes and dumped her in the two foot grave he'd prepared earlier. He took out a steak knife he'd lifted from the dining room and slashed her arm hoping the smell of fresh blood would attract any hungry predators. With any luck, they'd eat the evidence. He covered her body with leaves and left her there to die." Tom leaned back in his chair. "Yeah, a perfect plan. Except for one thing."

"What was that?" Jane asked sarcastically.

"The drowning hadn't kill her. It had only rendered her unconscious."

"So, in other words, she didn't die and there's really no point to this story. Am I right?"

"Oh, but she did die Jane," Katherine piped up. "She died of hypothermia, not at the hands of her husband."

"How is that possible?" Jane asked.

Tom rose to his full height of six foot four. "While the young woman lay there unconscious, and soaked to the skin, a bitter North wind blew the leaves from her body and she froze to death."

"So what's your point?"

"Well, every October right around this time," Tom smiled, "when there's a chill in the air, like there is tonight, she shows up."

"Where?" Jane laughed. "Around your little bonfire?"

"No, in someone's bedroom," Tom replied. "We just never know whose." He turned to his next door neighbor. "She was at your place last year wasn't she, Mae?"

"Oh, yes," Mae Bellman exclaimed. "She took the patch work quilt my granddaughter gave me for my birthday."

Jane looked at the woman as if she were from Mars. "You're kidding, right?"

"Oh, no dear. Every year on the anniversary of her death she visits someone's cottage and takes a blanket. I assume it's to keep herself warm."

Jane abruptly stood up. "This is ridiculous. I'm going to bed." She turned and looked down at Ben. "Are you coming?"

"You go ahead. I'll be up in a minute," Ben smiled. "I just want to say goodnight to everyone."

Tom called after Jane as she stormed up the hill. "Have a good night and don't forget, we're going fishing at 05:00."

At two in morning, the blanket covering Jane's naked body

began moving. "Ben, you're being a cover hog," she mumbled as she rolled over and felt for his warmth. When she discovered she was alone, she opened her eyes and watched in horror as the quilt lifted off the bed, rose above her feet, and slowly moved towards the open bedroom door.

The first sound heard by Tom, Katherine and Ben was Jane's horrifying scream. The second was the roar of her car engine as she pulled out of the driveway. It was the last time she and Ben dated.

***

Ben locked the truck and headed across the parking lot to the fire hall. He was glad Rachel had a sense of humor. When he, Tom and Katherine pulled the same prank on her last month, she'd laughed about it for week.

"Rachel, Rachel, wherefore art thou Rachel," Ben exclaimed into the cool night air. He'd only been away from her for half an hour and he missed her all ready.

He knew she was the best thing that had happened to him. She understood what he did for a living. She dealt with his job, and knew there were times when he just needed to be left alone. Times when he needed to mull over the call that went sideways, or the child he couldn't save.

Ben wasn't surprised that Rachel had done so well for herself, she'd always been motivated. When they first reconnected six months ago, he learned that during the short time she'd lived in Seattle, she'd made quite a name for herself in the commercial real estate market.

Rachel was an intelligent, beautiful woman both inside and out. She gave of her time freely and never refused to help out with a fire department fundraiser. Generous to a fault, last month when she discovered that the reception hall Sarah and Billy had booked for their Christmas Eve wedding burned to the ground, her generosity shifted into overdrive.

"Sarah, my father may be dead," Rachel had told her, "but his name still holds a lot of clout in the hotel business. Let me see what I can do."

***

When Ben walked through the front door of Fire Hall No. 19, to relieve Tom, the tones were going off throughout the hall.

"Evening, Captain. Your timing couldn't be better," Scott Tanaka, tonight's nozzle man smiled from the door of the alarm room.

"I can hear that," Ben nodded. "What have we got?"

"I didn't hear all of the dispatch, but No. 12's going in first. We're just the second-string on this one."

Within seconds of the alarm, Lieutenant, Brian Brooks, Firefighters Gord Wheaton, Greg Bishop and Ted Brown had joined the two men.

"Where's Tom," Ben asked.

"He's in the kitchen," Brian told him.

"Great. I'll just go drop this off and relieve him. I'll be back in minute." Ben headed down the hall with a spring in his step. Rachel had accepted his proposal. Life was good.

"You look like you're in a good mood buddy," Tom chuckled as Ben bounced into the kitchen.

"I sure am," Ben smiled back. "Couldn't be better."

"That must mean that Rachel said yes."

"She sure did," Ben replied with a beaming grin. He motioned to the alarm room. "You want me to take the call?"

"Nah," Tom smiled, "go have a shower and change. I'll take it. We shouldn't be that long. Coffee when we get back would be nice."

"But I promised Katherine, that I'd have you home by 21:30 and according to the clock on the wall, you're late. She'll have my ass."

Tom gave Ben a friendly pat on the shoulder. "Don't worry about Katherine. When I tell her why you were late, she'll start planning the wedding. Besides, she's waited this long to celebrate our twenty-fifth anniversary in Maui, a little while longer won't kill her. Go upstairs and have a shower. I'm sure we won't be long."

Chapter Twenty Nine

AS CAPTAIN TOM CHAMBERS and the crew from No. 19 raced towards the call they listened to the exchange of information between Engine Company No. 12 and dispatch.

"Dispatch, this is No. 12. Can we get an update on that fire."

"Engine Company 12, this is dispatch. We have confirmed reports of smoke showing at that address."

"Ten-four dispatch."

Tom knew the crew from No. 12 would be coming in from the north. With reports of smoke showing, they'd grab a hydrant on their way in. Tom would take his crew and pick up a hydrant on the south side of the street

"Dispatch, this is No. 12. We've arrived on scene. This is a three-floor, twelve-suite, walk-up apartment building. We have smoke showing. We're gonna pick up a hydrant and assume command at the front of the building. My guys are taking hand lines and going in to start a primary search. I need more manpower and another tac channel."

Tom picked up the radio attached to the dashboard of the engine. "No. 12 command, this is No. 19. We're coming in from the south. Where do you want us?" He asked.

"Grab the hydrant on Barlow and James. Meet me at the front of the building and tie into our engine," Gerry Kirkland, No. 12's Captain responded.

"Ten-four."

"When you're geared up Tom," Gerry continued, "take charge of sector one. My guys are already inside with lines. They're on tac channel three.

"Ten-four," Tom replied as the rig from No. 19 pulled into position.

The men quickly masked up and headed to the front of the apartment. As Tom, Garth and Scott were about to enter the building, a frazzled woman pushed her way through the crowd of spectators. She frantically raced up the front stairs screaming, "my kids, my kids are inside!"

Tom grabbed her by the arm as she tried to run past him. "How many kids?" he asked.

"Two, I have two. Oh my God, they're going to burn!"

The woman tried to pull free but Tom turned her towards him. "Where's your apartment?" he asked.

"On the second floor." She pointed skyward. "Up there, on the second floor. Apartment 201."

"Are your kids in the apartment?"

The woman shook her head in confusion. "I don't know," she cried. "They were there when I left for the store fifteen minutes ago, but I left the door open. They could be anywhere."

"How old are they?" Tom asked.

"Three and five. The kids are three and five."

Tom hit the button on his radio. "Incident command. This is search sector one. We have a situation. We have a woman here, she has two kids inside. I'm taking my guys and going up to apartment 201 to do a search." He flipped the dial on his radio to tac channel three and contacted the crew inside. "Sector one, this is Captain Chambers, where are you?"

"Checking the third floor," a voice replied.

"We have a report of two kids in apartment 201. I'm taking my crew and going up to investigate. When you're finished with your search on third floor, check the second floor. Chambers out."

"Ten-four," a voice replied.

Tom turned to Scott and Gord. "You ready to go boys?"

"Ready when you are," Scott replied.

"Okay, let's do it. We're on tac channel twelve."

The men turned the dials on their radios, pulled their facemasks into place, and headed into the smoke. Tom knew from the pre-plan map that the historical three-floor walk up could be a death trap. The apartment was built years ago using a form of construction know as ballooning. The exterior walls of the building were constructed in one solid piece from the ground up. The floors had no support except for the plates they rested on. The plates were attached to the sills on the building's exterior walls.

When Tom, Scott and Gord reached apartment 201, the door was open. They stepped across the threshold and the floor gave slightly under their weight. The fire was burning directly below them. There wouldn't be a floor much longer. All three firefighters knew that they shouldn't go any further; it wasn't safe under such unstable conditions, but there were lives at stake – children's lives – and there was nothing more important to a firefighter than saving the life of a child!

To distribute their weight more evenly, the three men got down on all fours. "Gord, I want you to go left. Search the kitchen, living room and dining room," Tom told him with the aid of his radio. "Scott, you take the bathroom and bedrooms. I'll stay at the door."

As quickly as they could, Scott and Gord crawled through the dense smoke in search of the missing children. In the kitchen, Gord opened all of the lower cupboards, the fridge, and the oven. He swept his hands under the table and checked the broom closet. When he found nothing, he crawled to the dining room.

In the bathroom, Scott checked under the sink, behind the toilet and in the tub. There were no signs of the children. He headed down the hall to the first bedroom. There, he looked on top and under the bed. He opened the doors of the night table and checked under the dresser. He found nothing in the closet or behind the drapes.

He moved to the second bedroom and repeated the process. Frustrated, he reached up and hit his mike button. "Tom, search completed in bathroom and bedrooms, nothing found. I'm coming back to you."

"Ten-four," Tom replied.

When Gord found nothing in the dining room he moved into the living room. He swept his arms over and under a chair and moved the footstool. The smoke was getting thicker and he blindly felt his way to the sofa. He threw the cushions on the floor and pulled the piece of furniture away from the wall. There, he found something. He quickly hit the button on his radio. "Captain, I've got something behind the couch. I need your help."

Tom reached for his radio. "Incident command, this is Captain Chambers. We believe we've found somebody in the living room. My partner and I are going in to help."

Tom released the mike button, then quickly hit it again. "Gord, Scott and I will be right there."

"Be careful," Gord radioed back. "I can feel the floor getting spongy."

The fire was burning hotter and all around them, the men could hear evidence of its raging anger. The building groaned and hissed as pieces of it gave into the destructive flames. Cautiously, Tom and Scott crawled through the thick smoke. When they reached Gord, he was pulling an object out from behind the couch. "Shit, he yelled. "It's not a kid, it's a damn stuffed animal."

"Can you find anything else?" Tom yelled through his mask.

Gord ran his gloved hands under the sofa. "I've got something." He pulled it out. It was a dead cat.

Tom reached for his mike button just as the floor started to rumble beneath his knees. "Incident command, this is Chambers. We have not found, I repeat, not found a casualty. We are abandoning our search, it isn't safe."

Tom grabbed the back of Scott's duty coat, gave it a tug, and pointed towards the front door. "We need to get out of here and fast," he yelled through his mask. "The floor's going to go!"

On hands and knees, the three men cautiously began inching backward across the living room. Five feet from the front door, the building started to rumble. Tom knew it wasn't a good sign. He grabbed for his radio. "Incident command evacuate all personnel. I repeat. Evacuate all personnel. It's not safe!"

Within seconds of the radio transmission from Captain Tom Chambers, the north side of the building collapsed.

Chapter Thirty

OUTSIDE, KATHERINE COULD HEAR the faint wail of sirens as fire trucks made their way to a call in the valley below. Occasionally, the sirens would send a wave of fear through her body, but not tonight. Tonight, Tom was home and she was lying in bed in the protection of his arms.

She raised herself up on one elbow and looked into her husband's hypnotic blue eyes. "Well Mr. Chambers, if all of our children's problems are solved and we don't have to worry about anyone else, perhaps we should just worry about us."

She felt his body tremble beneath her as her moist tongue playfully darted back and forth across his chest. She straddled him and pushed his arms out to his side. With a feather touch, she seductively slid her fingertips across Tom's broad shoulders and continued moving down the muscular curves of his arms until they found his strong powerful hands.

Katherine loved Tom's hands, their size, their shape, everything about them. They were strong hands, rugged hands. Hands that proudly displayed a scar or two from carpentry projects over the years. They were hands of knowledge, their lines and calluses showing what they had learned through years of use. But most of all, they were the gentle hands that had protected, cared for, and caressed her for the past twenty-five years.

She brought Tom's fingers to her lips and circled the tip of each one with her tongue. She kissed his palm, and nibbled her way up his arm from his wrist to his elbow. When he let out a boyish giggle, she pinned his arms at his side and entwined her fingers in his. She bent downwards until her face was nestled in his chest.

Tom let out a satisfying moan as Katherine's tongue traveled towards his navel. "You're driving me crazy," he whispered.

"You haven't seen anything yet my love," she whispered back.

As Katherine moved towards Tom's growing desire, she was sure she heard the front door bell. *Someone has really lousy timing*, Katherine told herself. "Don't answer it. They'll go away."

She pulled up the covers and wrapped her arms around her head in a desperate attempt to eliminate the annoying sound, but the bell kept ringing and ringing. When she couldn't stand it anymore, Katherine yanked the covers from her head and sat up. She was shocked, to discover that the room was pitch black. *I don't remember turning off the lights*, she thought.

A strange feeling swept over her and for a moment she wasn't sure where she was. She felt around the bed searching for the warmth of Tom's body but he wasn't there. She was alone in the darkness. Katherine rubbed the sleep from her eyes and leaned over to check the clock. The glowing red numbers indicated that it was 2:48 in the morning.

In the background, the annoying sound of the doorbell was now accompanied by intense knocking. Katherine searched the night table for the lamp and turned it on. Squinting to protect her eyes from the glare, she stumbled to the chair and grabbed her silk robe. "Tom. Where are you?" she called out as she marched down the stairs.

At the front entrance, Katherine flicked on the porch light and flung the door open without looking through the peephole. "What the hell do you want?" she barked before taking notice of who was standing on the front steps.

When her eyes finally focused and her mind registered she felt the blood drain from her face. There, stood Chief Riley and Chaplain Douglas. Their eyes saddened and filled with pain.

Katherine's legs went weak. She knew the only time a firefighter's wife got a visit from the Chief and the Chaplain was when something was wrong.

She closed her eyes. *I must be dreaming. They aren't here because of Tom,* she reassured herself. *Tom is home.* Satisfied with the explanation she'd given herself, Katherine opened her eyes. She expected to find herself nestled beside Tom in bed. Much to her dismay, she was still at the front door; the two gloomy faces staring back at her.

"May we come in, Katherine?" Chief Riley asked.

Katherine stepped back from the doorway. "Yes, of course. Please forgive my manners gentlemen, it's just that it's so late." Katherine motioned towards the living room. "Please, make yourselves at home. I'll just go and find Tom."

As she turned to walk away, the Chief reached out and gently grabbed her by the arm. "Katherine wait. Tom isn't here."

"Well, of course, he's here," she snapped. Her emotions now wrestling with her common sense, she yanked her arm from his grip. "What are you talking about? Tom's here. He's been home for hours."

"Katherine, please believe me, Tom isn't here."

"Yes he is," she argued. "We were just together. He must be in the bathroom."

Katherine glared at the Chief. Tears were forming in his eyes. Her stomach gave a heave and for a moment she thought she might be sick. Her hands started trembling, her head started spinning. *I couldn't have dreamt that Tom and I were just together*, she told herself. *Everything seemed so real.*

Her frightened eyes anxiously darted back and forth between the Chief and the Chaplain. Her chest tightened and she felt panic setting in. "What's going on?" She asked in a whisper. "Where's my husband? Where's Tom?"

Chaplain Douglas took Katherine by the arm. "Come." He led her to the sofa and sat down beside her. "Katherine, Tom is at the hospital."

"But what is he doing at the hospital?"

"There's been an accident," he told her.

"What do you mean there has been an accident? Was Tom in a car accident on his way home?"

"It wasn't a car accident Katherine. There's been a fire," Chief Riley quietly added.

The color drained from her face. "Oh my God. The phone call."

The Chief gave her a puzzled look. "What phone call?"

"The phone call. The phone call I got from Tom, just after nine." Her voice began trembling. "I heard alarm bells going off in the background just as I hung up."

Suddenly the visit from these two men was becoming all too clear. Something was wrong. She could feel it in her bones. "Has something happened to Tom?" Katherine asked in a whisper.

Chaplain Curtis took her hand in his and looked into her eyes. "Katherine, Tom is at the hospital. We need you to come with us."

Chapter Thirty One

KATHERINE GOT DRESSED AND the two men ushered her out to the van. On the way to the hospital, Fire Chief Jack Riley explained what had happened.

"Katherine, Tom's crew was called to an apartment fire just after nine-thirty. They were going in to back up No. 12. That would explain the alarms you mentioned hearing. The fire started in a ground floor corner suite. The owner wasn't home. When Tom and ..."

"Was it arson?" Katherine interrupted.

The Chief gave her a puzzled look. "Why would you ask such a question?"

"Come on Jack. How many firefighters have we lost this year? I'll tell you how many we've lost, six including Tom, Scott and Gord." Anger rose in her voice. "Three, of those six, were killed in arson related fires. I think it's a perfectly normal question. Did my husband die at the hand of an arsonist?"

"They haven't confirmed it was arson," Jack told her, "but by the burn patterns and the way it was going when No. 12 arrived, we're sure it was."

Katherine took a deep breath and fought to hold back the tears. "Please, continue. I'm sorry. I didn't mean to interrupt," she apologized.

"No need to apologize," the Chief smiled. "I can understand your concern. Anyway, when Tom and his crew arrived, the captain from No. 12 had taken command and his crew was inside with attack lines. Tom was advised, there may be children in the apartment directly above the fire. They knew it may not be safe, but Tom, Gord and Scott went in to look for the missing children anyway.

"They had completed their search and Tom had just advised command that they were leaving the apartment when the north side of the building collapsed."

"Did they find the children?" Katherine asked.

Jack lowered his head. "No," he quietly replied. "They didn't find any children."

How was he going to tell this woman, and the wives of the other firefighters, that there had never been any children in the apartment? The kids the frantic tenant spoke of were her two cats. Three good men were dead. Three women were widows and several children had lost a parent. It was a tragedy that never should have happened.

"Jack, you mentioned that part of the building collapsed. Were did they find Tom and his crew? Were they buried alive?"

"No." The Chief shifted nervously in his seat. "I don't think we really need to go into this now, Katherine. Do we?"

"Yes, we do," she firmly stated. "I need to know exactly what happened so I can tell my children."

Chief Riley took a deep breath. "Tom went down first."

"Did he only fall one floor?" Katherine asked.

"Yes," the Chief replied.

"Did the fall kill him?"

"The paramedics don't think so."

"Then what did?"

"Katherine, I really don't think we should be discussing this. If it's of that much interest to you, you're welcome to come to the de-briefing."

"For Christ's sake Jack," Katherine snapped, "just tell me what the hell happened. What killed my husband, Scott and Gord?"

The Chief cleared his throat. "Tom went down first. Gord landed on top of him. The impact broke Tom's neck."

"What happened to Gord and Scott?" Katherine asked, more concerned now about Wendy Wheaton and Sandra Tanaka, the two men's wives. They would be absolutely devastated. Sandra Tanaka had just come over from Japan and spoke very little English. The poor woman would have no idea what was going on. Wendy Wheaton was expecting a baby. Katherine hoped the news wouldn't put her into premature labor.

"Gord landed on top of Tom's air tank," the Chief continued. "The impact shattered his chest."

"And Scott, what happened to Scott?"

"He fell from the second floor to the basement. His back broke on impact with the concrete floor."

"How long did it take you to get them out?" Katherine asked in a calm, quiet voice.

"The heavy rescue from No. 9 arrived five minutes after they were dispatched. It took them three hours to shore up the building before it was safe for anyone to go inside."

"What time did the fire start?"

"The call was received by No. 19 at 21:38."

"What time did the men die?"

"We received Tom's last transmission at 22:01. The floor collapsed only seconds later."

Katherine took a deep breath. "Thank you, Jack. I know it wasn't easy for you to tell me all this, but I needed to know."

When the Chief's van pulled up in front of the hospital, Ben was waiting at the front door. Katherine watched him as he walked toward the vehicle. For a brief instant, she hated him. He was supposed to have been at the hall at nine to relieve Tom. If he had been, Tom would still be alive. She wouldn't be here at the hospital to say goodbye to her husband – she would be getting on a plane with him to celebrate their twenty-fifth anniversary in Maui.

She wouldn't have to phone her children and tell them that their father was dead. She wouldn't have to call Tom's father and tell him that he'd lost his only son. She wouldn't have to go through the rest of her life alone.

Ben opened the van door and helped Katherine out of the vehicle. "Oh, Katherine," he pulled her into his arms, "how can I ever make this up to you. I should have been at the hall at nine like I promised. If I had, Tom would still be alive."

Katherine started to cry. The hate she'd felt for this man only moments ago vanished. "Oh, Ben," she sobbed. "It's not your fault. Please don't blame yourself."

"But Katherine, I promised you I'd be at the hall by nine. I was late. If I would have been on time, you and Tom would be going in there to see me," Ben motioned over his shoulder towards the building, "not the other way around. That's the way it should have been, Katherine. You and Tom have kids. I don't."

Tears streamed down Ben's face and Katherine pulled him closer. "Ben, please don't do this. Death is a hazard of the job. You know that, I know that and Tom knew that when he got into the engine to go to the call."

Chapter Thirty Two

CHARLIE BENSON, THE CHAMBERS' family physician and close personal friend dropped Katherine off at the house just as the sun was coming up. He'd given her a sedative to help her sleep but it hadn't worked and now her mind was as foggy as it had been when she had left in the middle of the night.

"Can I get you a cup of coffee?" Rachel asked.

Katherine offered her friend a sad smile. "'Thanks. That would be great." For a long moment she stood in silence staring out the window. The sky was gray. It had started to rain. Her heart sank as she looked towards the Pacific. *Ben should be taking Tom and I to the airport right now,* she thought. The tears came quickly and she reached into the pocket of her terry robe for a handkerchief.

"Here's your coffee Kate. Let's sit down for awhile and then I'll make you something to eat." Rachel escorted her to the kitchen table and pulled out a chair.

Katherine sat down and her hands shook as she accepted the mug of steaming black liquid. "Thank you Rachel, and thank you for being here. It really means a lot to me."

"Don't mention it," Rachel smiled. "I wouldn't be anywhere else. You know that."

Katherine stared at the newspaper on the table in front of her. "Is there anything about it in the Tribune?"

"Yes," Rachel reluctantly answered. "It's in the City Section." Slowly, Katherine reached across the table and pulled the morning newspaper towards her. She slowly unfolded it and thumbed through each section until she found the article she was looking for.

"I'll get that," Rachel announced at the sound of the telephone.

"Thanks," Katherine smiled, "and unless it's someone from the fire department, Ben, my kids, or my mother, I don't want to talk to them."

"Hello. This is the Chambers residence," Rachel answered in a pleasant voice. "How may I help you?" There was a long silent pause. "No, I'm sorry. Mrs. Chambers isn't able to come to the telephone right now."

"Who is it?" Katherine asked.

Rachel put her hand over the mouthpiece. "It's Jane Phillips. She wants to talk to you."

"About what?"

"An interview, I think."

"Tell her I'm not interested in talking to her."

"Ms. Phillips," Rachel began. "I'm afraid that now is not a good time." There was a pause. "No, she won't be able to call you back in an hour."

Katherine stood up from the kitchen table and walked to the desk. "Give me the phone. I'll talk to her."

Rachel covered the mouthpiece with her hand. "Are you sure? You really don't have to do this right now."

"If I don't talk to her now, she'll drive me crazy until I do. She's a reporter!" Katherine took the receiver from Rachel's hand. "Hello, Jane. This is Katherine. How can I help you?"

Katherine listened for a few minutes before responding. "No, Jane, I have no comment at this time on the fact that my husband, and two of his crew members, died last night trying to save the lives of two cats, that he was told were kids." She took a deep breath to fight back the tears. "I don't mean to be rude, Jane, but I really can't talk right now. If you have any questions, I'd appreciate it if you'd call Mark Turner."

Katherine hung up the phone and walked back to the kitchen table. She stared down at the open newspaper and tears streamed down her face as she tried to read the article.

Fire Captain Tom Chambers and two of his crewmembers, Nozzle Man Scott Tanaka and First Class Firefighter Gord Wheaton perished last night when the building they were in collapsed...

Chapter Thirty Three

THE FIRE DEPARTMENT MADE all of the arrangements for one of the largest funerals the city had every seen. The mayor declared a day of mourning and thousands of people attended the service.

Mourners, who couldn't find space in the cathedral, lined the street and listened over the loud speaker as the Chief honored the three men by reading the firefighters prayer.

In addition to each firefighter's eulogy, a member of their bereaved family had been asked to say a few words and share a favorite story of the deceased; something that would help everyone remember the fallen firefighter with a smile. Katherine asked Ben to do the honors.

Ben stared out at the sea of black that rippled through the pews like a wave. It had been a very difficult day. It had been a difficult week. Katherine's son, Matthew, was devastated by his father's death and refused to fly home for the funeral. He wanted no part of it. Ben talked to him until he was blue in the face, but to no avail. Matthew was like his mother; once he'd made up his mind about something, there was no changing it.

Matthew's sister Samantha, on the other hand, was being a brave solider. Ben knew that she was suffering in silence. Katherine was also becoming a concern. Since Tom's death, she'd given all of her time to Sandra Tanaka trying to help her cope with the tragedy of Scott's death.

Ben himself had lost his best friend to arson, six months after losing a crewmember to the same thing. At least, they'd thought Michael Wells died because of the Brandon Furniture

Store fire. Rachel had a different version. Two weeks ago when she was attending Sarah Baker's bridal shower she overhead a telephone conversation Jane Phillips was having.

***

"I don't care what the paper said," Jane told her listener. "Michael Wells didn't die from the injuries he sustained in that fire. He was murdered. How do I know? I'll tell you how I know. I ran into Doctor Hanson in the hospital cafeteria last week. Yeah, the same Doctor Hanson, the good-looking one. Anyway, he told me, off the record, that Michael died from a saddle embolus in his pulmonary artery. The toxicology screen revealed traces of Valium and lactose in his blood.

***

Ben shook the conversation from his mind and took a sip of water to relieve his dry throat. "Ladies and gentleman," he began. "I've been asked to share a story with you. It was one of Tom's favorites.

"As most of you know, Fire Captain Tom Chambers had a wonderful sense of humor, and although his Fire Watch lottery has duped a lot of rookies over the years, it has also raised thousands of dollars for our Children's Hospital. Well, Tom was duped himself a time or two."

Ben smiled at his audience. "Tom began his firefighting career in Ottawa, Canada. Four years after becoming a city firefighter, he saw a job posting that caught his eye. The dive team was looking for candidates. Having previous diving experience, Tom jumped at the chance. He took the course, passed the exams and transferred to Fire Hall No. 6.

"Being the new guy on the crew, the rookie you might say, Tom's first responsibility was to maintain the boat. He polished the chrome, scrubbed the hull, and treated it like it was his favorite sports car.

"One sunny Sunday afternoon, only two weeks after being

stationed at his new hall, he got his first water rescue call. Someone reported seeing a body in the river. Tom thought it was strange that he hadn't heard the call come in, but he erased it from his mind, grabbed his gear and jumped into the driver's seat of the pick-up. With his lieutenant at his side, they raced out of the hall and up the highway towards the river.

"Ten minutes into the ride, the lieutenant looked at Tom and asked, 'Where's the boat?' When Tom glanced in the rear-view mirror all he saw was an empty trailer. The boat was gone.

"For half an hour, Tom's lieutenant made him drive up and down the highway in search of the water rescue craft. When they couldn't find it, he ordered him back to the hall."

Ben leaned closer to the podium. "As you can well imagine, Tom was beside himself. He'd just put the biggest black mark on his record that anyone could possible put there. He knew there would be an investigation and he was sure he'd lose his job. If he did, how would he support his new family?

"When they got back to the hall, the captain called Tom into the office and tore a strip off of him. He told him how irresponsible he'd been and because of his irresponsibility a life had been lost.

"The captain informed Tom that a by-stander had pulled the body from the river and it was waiting for him in the ambulance on the apparatus floor. He ordered Tom to ride with the body to the hospital and explain to the boy's family why their son was dead."

A hush fell over the room and behind her, Katherine heard someone whisper. "This is the most ridiculous thing I've ever heard. Why would Katherine let Ben stand up there and tell a story like this? Personally, I think it's disgusting talking about her dead husband's responsibility for someone's death."

A grin found its way to Katherine's face. She wasn't offended by the remark – there was no reason to be. She loved this story. It had been one of her husband's favorites.

"Tom followed his captain's orders and headed to the ambulance," Ben continued. "As he walked past the men of his crew, he was ashamed to call himself a firefighter. He was a disgrace to the profession! He was a disgrace to mankind! He'd killed someone out of his own stupidity. He was sure he fastened the boat securely after he washed it. Obviously, he hadn't.

"The paramedics opened the door of the ambulance and Tom climbed up the steps. Inside, lying on the gurney, was a body covered with a white sheet, a toe tag hung from the victim's left foot. Tom told me he felt sick. He'd taken away someone's son, someone's boyfriend, and someone's brother.

"In a needed to know moment, Tom reached for the toe tag. As he took it in his hand to examine it, the body sat up." A loud gasp broke the silence of the church. "Well, Tom shot out of the bus and by the time he landed, Glen King, the body on the gurney, was standing overtop of him laughing like crazy."

Ben started to laugh and soon the entire congregation laughed along with him. "It had all been an elaborate plan," Ben went on to explain. "The crew had jacked up the boat three inches so that when Tom left, he'd leave without it. While Tom and his lieutenant were gone, the guys put the boat on the spare trailer and moved it to the back parking lot.

"When Tom and his lieutenant got back to the hall, Tom's crew convinced him that the victim had drowned. In actual fact, there'd never been a victim at all. The whole thing had been a big joke." Ben paused until the wave of laugher quieted. "Tom, had been had and according to him, it was the best practical joke he'd ever been witness to."

As Ben stepped from the microphone, he knew that his story had changed the tears and sorrow of the congregation to laughter. He'd accomplished his mission. Tom Chambers would be proud.

The next person to speak was Kevin Wheaton, Gord's older brother. " My brother was only a firefighter for three years," he began, "but he loved his job and he loved working with Tom and the crew at Fire Hall No. 19.

"As you've just heard, Captain Chambers had a great sense of humor and my brother often talked about the onion ring incident.

"Apparently, Gord mentioned to Captain Chambers one

day that he really liked onion rings and Tom told him he would have Scott whip him up a special batch.

"Well, lunchtime rolled around and when Gord walked into the kitchen, as promised, he found a huge plate of onion rings waiting for him. He offered to share them with the crew, but they all declined. He grabbed one, popped it into his mouth and started to chew. Well, he chewed and chewed and chewed. He told me he had no idea what he was eating, but he was sure it wasn't an onion ring.

"He found out later that it wasn't! According to my brother, when you dip half-inch rubber bands in batter and deep fry them, they look pretty much the same!"

The last person to speak was Fire Department Public Information Officer, Mark Turner. "The Tanaka family has asked me to share a story with you. It's not a practical joke, but it was an incident that Scott often laughed about when he was sharing a beer with the boys at the Hose and Hydrant.

"The event, as Scott liked to call it, happened six years ago when he was stationed at Fire Hall No. 20. The crew was called to a townhouse fire. When they got there, one of the neighbors came running up to the rig and told Scott to watch out for snakes. Apparently, the children that lived in the house raised them.

"Scott and his partner grabbed a hose line and went inside. By the time they got to the back bedroom, they couldn't see more than two feet in front of them. When Scott shone his flashlight around room, he discovered that the walls were lined with glass aquariums. He was sure, they were all occupied by snakes and thankful that they had lids. Scott hated snakes," Mark smiled, "and he often commented that he'd walk across water to avoid one."

A murmur of laughter rolled through the crowd. "As Scott told the story," Mark continued, "he shone his flashlight up at the ceiling only to discover that it was crawling with snakes. He figured he must have screamed, because his partner hit the ceiling with a fog pattern from the hose and the snakes started dropping like flies.

"It was at that point ladies and gentleman, that Scott Tanaka, one of our fearless firefighter's dropped his flashlight, covered his head with his hands, and ran out of the room like a frightened little boy!" A grin danced across Mark's face. "Scott always laughed about this episode. Especially when he found out that what he thought were live snakes, were only their skins."

"Thank you Lieutenant," Reverend Douglas smiled. "Ladies and gentleman that concludes our service. The bodies of Fire Captain Tom Chambers, Nozzle Man Scott Tanaka and First Class Firefighter Gordon Wheaton will now be transported to their final resting-place. There will be a short service at the graveside and then you are all invited to join the families at the union hall for a light lunch."

Chapter Thirty Four

THE FIRE DEPARTMENT UNION hall was filled to capacity with uniformed firefighters, civilians, and police officers all offering their condolences.

"Thanks, Rachel. I need this," Katherine smiled as she accepted the steaming cup of coffee.

"The ladies did a great job of setting up the lunch," Rachel remarked as she looked around the room. "I hope they have enough sandwiches. I can't believe the number of people here."

"Firefighter funerals are always like this," Katherine told her, "and to be perfectly honest with you, I'm getting tired of going to them." She took a sip of her coffee. "Oh, by the way, have you heard anything from Michael Wells' mother?"

"Why would I hear from Michael Wells' mother?" Rachel asked defensively.

"Oh, I don't mean you personally," Katherine chuckled. "I just thought that perhaps Ben may have heard from her."

"No, no he hasn't."

"Mrs. Chambers, excuse me. My name is Kurt Roper. I work for the Tribune. I don't mean to interrupt, and I know this may not be the best time, but I just wanted to offer you my condolences on the recent loss of you husband." He stuck out his chubby little hand.

"I'm pleased to meet you Mr. Roper. Did you know my husband?"

Kurt's face turned red. "No. No I didn't." He reached into his coat pocket and felt for the security of his silver booze flask.

"Did you know one of the other men?"

Kurt cleared his throat. "No Mrs. Chambers, I didn't know any of the firefighters personally, but I just feel awful about this."

"We all do," Katherine replied. "It's a tragic loss."

"Mrs. Chambers, it was my apartment where the fire originally started. I only wish I'd have been home. Maybe I could have prevented this from happening, but I was at the nursing home caring for my ailing mother. You have no idea how badly I feel. I had no idea the building would collapse."

"Thank you very much Mr. Roper, but you have nothing to feel bad about. Tom was just doing his job and he always knew there were risks involved."

"I realize that, but I never wanted this to happen. I never wanted anyone to get hurt."

Katherine flashed him a puzzled look. "What do you mean you never wanted anyone to get hurt?"

Kurt bounced nervously from foot to foot. "Oh, it's nothing. You can be sure the arson division will find the person responsible. In fact, they might very well be examining a lead at this very minute." Kurt thought about the tape and the file he'd left in the safe. He hadn't heard from anyone, but he was sure the fire department would have found the evidence by now. If they hadn't, when they did, Jane would be going to jail.

"How do you know it was arson," Ben interrupted as he joined in the conversation.

"Well, ah, I've," Kurt stammered, "I've got connections with the cops. Now if you'll excuse me." He turned on his heels and disappeared into the crowd.

"That was strange," Ben remarked as he watched the funny little man walk away. "What did he want?"

"He just wanted to offer his condolences. Apparently, the fire that killed Tom, Scott and Gord started in Mr. Roper's apartment." Katherine dabbed at her nose with the Kleenex she'd been clutching in her hand. "Can we please talk about something happier. I've had my fill of arson fires."

"I'm sorry." Ben apologized.

Katherine glanced across the room and saw Sarah walking

towards her. "Speaking of something happier, here comes the bride. She smiled and patted the empty chair beside her. "Sit down Sarah. Let's talk about your wedding plans."

"Katherine, I'm just going to take Rachel over and introduce her to someone. We'll be back in a minute. Will you be okay?"

"Yes." Katherine smiled up at Ben and Rachel. "Take your time. I'm not going anywhere. I'm just going to sit here and have a nice chat with Sarah."

She turned her attention back to the attractive young woman now sitting beside her. "So are you getting excited?"

"Oh, yes," Sarah beamed. "Counting down the weeks. I don't know what I would have done without all the help you and Rachel have given me. When our reception hall burned down, I had no idea what I was going to do. I figured the most special day of Billy's and my life was ruined. I can't believe, that now, I'm getting married in a beautiful old hotel in the heart of the Canadian Rockies." Sarah's smile suddenly faded. "Oh my God!" She exclaimed. Something just occurred to me."

"What's that dear?" Katherine asked.

"How am I going to get the wedding party to the wedding? Billy and I can't afford to fly everyone to Canada!"

"Oh, I guess Rachel hasn't had a chance to talk to you yet."

"Talk to me about what?" Sarah asked.

"Well, it appears, that her boss has offered his private jet, so you don't have to worry your pretty little head about a thing."

Sarah started to cry and threw her arms around Katherine's neck. "How can I ever repay both of you for all you've done?"

"You don't have to repay us dear. We're just glad we can help. Personally, I appreciate you letting me be your stand-in mother."

"You're welcome," Sarah sniffled. "I'm glad to have you as a stand-in mother." She wiped the tears from her cheeks. "I suppose you'll have to do the same thing for Rachel when she and Ben get married."

"Yes, I suppose I will," Katherine grinned, "but before any weddings take place, I need to get through the gala next week."

Sarah gave Katherine a puzzled look. "I thought they were going to cancel the gala because of the fire.

"They already postponed it once, dear. When Michael Wells died. Don't you remember? Anyway, I told the chief that Tom wouldn't have approved. He loved the gala and he always had a great time."

Sarah's body gave a shiver when Michael's name rolled off Katherine's tongue. She hated Michael. She'd hated him for years. Since finding out from Rachel that the fire hadn't killed Michael, Sarah was positive she had. Every night since then, the same image haunted her mind. As if watching from above, she saw herself gliding into Michael's hospital room. She'd stand beside the bed. She'd tell him she was going to kill him, then she'd load the syringe.

Katherine gave Sarah a shake. "Are you okay?" She asked, as she watched the color drain from the young woman's face. "I seem to have lost you there for a moment."

"I'm sorry. Did you say something?"

"Are you okay?" Katherine asked. "You look like you've just seen a ghost."

Chapter Thirty Five

SHE PULLED THE BENCH from under the antique dressing table and sat down. For ten minutes, she examined the face staring back at her. It had changed over the years. The buckteeth of her adolescence had been replaced with a pearly white porcelain dental bridge. Her new smile, a fifteenth birthday present compliments of her Uncle Henry.

"At least that's one decent gift you gave me that year," she told her reflection as she examined her crowns. "Your other present almost destroyed my life." She closed her eyes and the image flashed before her like a horror film.

***

The room was pitch black, but she knew she wasn't alone. She could smell the stale smoke on his clothes from the fire he'd just put out. "Where are you kitten?" He asked. "I want to give you your present."

As quietly as she could, she slid from under the covers, dropped to the floor and hid beneath the bed. If Henry couldn't find her, maybe he'd go away.

"Now, don't be shy. You've got the body of an eighteen-year-old. Let me show you how to use it. Trust me kid, someday it'll come in handy."

For years, the emotions and hatred of his weekly visits swirled inside her like the dangerous gases and volatile combustible substances in a fire. When she turned seventeen, she reached her flashpoint.

She was positive the only reason Henry insisted she take a job at his lodge that summer, was so he could keep an eye on her. He'd caught her in bed with Jeremy Watson, and after giving the eighteen-year-old football star the thrashing of his life, Henry locked her in her room.

"I'll let you out when you hump me, like you humped that scrawny little blonde-haired, blue eyed, football faggot."

It was the straw that broke the camel's back. She spent three days in her room with no food or water. On the fourth day, after concocting a brilliant plan to get rid of dear old Uncle Henry, once and for all, she gave into his demands.

"Now, give it to me like you gave it to that kid, and I'll show you what it's like to ride a real stallion, not a colt."

"You want to go for a ride, Henry?" She masked her hatred with a seductive smile and straddled his grotesque overweight body. "Well, take a deep seat and a far-away look because I'm going to give you the ride of your life."

Her body moved in rhythm to his, and with each thrust of his loins, her loathing for the man grew stronger. When he was finished, she couldn't wait to kill him.

That night, she set fire to her uncle's room and launched her career in arson.

***

She shook off the sickening reminder of her teens and picked up the sterling silver hairbrush that once belonged to her mother. "One, two, three," she counted as she stroked her long silky hair. At fifty strokes, she stopped. "There Momma, fifty strokes just like you taught me."

She missed not having a mother while growing up, but her mother's sister had been a fairly decent replacement. Aunt Hazel always treated her like one of her own. She was a wonderful, kind woman. Too bad she'd had such lousy taste in husbands.

She'd never liked her Uncle Henry. Neither had her grandfather, at first. Henry was an American. Grandfather was a staunch Brit; he didn't like Americans. Unfortunately, when he discovered that Henry was a firefighter, he changed his mind.

"I had friends on London's fire brigade during the Second World War," he'd said. "They were proud, honorable men, who helped save the city from Hitler's bombs. Some of them were Americans. If Henry's a firefighter, he can't be all bad."

Henry may have had a respectable job, and earned the respect of her grandfather, but in her eyes, he wasn't a respectable man. He was a womanizer, something she discovered the first time she met him. It was in London at her grandmother's house. Granny was throwing an elaborate engagement party for Aunt Hazel. While her aunt was in the kitchen, Henry was in the garden with one of the female servants.

Henry was no gentleman, he was a wolf in sheep's clothing and she'd never trusted him. She was positive he'd only married her aunt for her money. When she overhead a conversation he was having with one of his buddies, her suspicions were confirmed: "I keep my job on the fire department, just so I can get away from the wife four days a week. I don't need to work, she's got millions and someday it will be mine. When I'm home, looking at that hot little niece of hers makes up for every time the ball and chain bitches at me."

Well, she'd taken care of Uncle Henry just like she'd taken care of the other firefighters. She wouldn't have had to kill them if they'd just kept their hands to themselves, but each one of them had been just like her uncle. They weren't interested in her mind. All that they were interested in was her body and the pleasure it could give them.

For years, she thought all firefighters were the same. Then she met the one who'd changed her mind. She picked up the picture of her fiancé and offered the handsome, proud firefighter a warm smile. "You're not like that, are you? You're not like Travis Greenwood or Michael Wells or Uncle Henry. You're not like the guy I did in Denver or the one in Boston. You're not like any of them." She set the picture back on the dresser and smiled. It had been a whirlwind romance, and for the first time in her life, she'd been swept off her feet. He was a wonderful man and she'd make him a wonderful wife.

She reached for the small sterling silver jewelry box and pulled it towards her. Slowly, she opened the lid and stared inside. "Only one more item and my collection will be complete."

A satisfied smile danced across her face as she reached inside. "First, something old." She picked up the fire department ring that once belonged to her Uncle Henry and set it in front of her. Next, she took out the Chicago Fire Department ring she'd been given when she was employed with the fire department in 1999. She rolled it over and over in her fingers. "Well, it isn't new, but it will have to do." She laughed at her poetic phrase and set the ring beside Henry's. The last item she retrieved from the tiny sterling silver jewel box was a gold fire department ring with a blue sapphire stone. It was the one she'd taken from Travis Greenwood when she set his apartment on fire. "Something old, something new and something blue. Almost perfect."

She reached under her long hair and unclasped the gold chain that hung from her neck. "You don't want to lose these," she told her reflection. One by one she slid the rings onto the chain to accompany the sparkling gem already hanging there. She re-fastened the necklace and tucked it under her turtleneck. She closed the box and slipped it into the top drawer.

She was positive that once the wedding band was on her finger, the nightmares of her youth would vanish. She would hang up her matches once and for all. First, there was something she needed to do. She had to set just one more fire. This time she wouldn't kill a firefighter. This time, she'd kill a so-called family friend.

Aaron Cook, her late father's ex-financial planner, was becoming a problem. She had no idea how he'd found the diary and videotapes she'd hidden at her father's ranch, but nonetheless, he'd found them. Now, he knew all about the fires and how she'd set them.

Aaron presented her with his envelope of evidence in New

York last month. He promised, if she got professional psychiatric help, he'd keep his mouth shut. She didn't believe him, why should she. He'd already taken her for a quarter of a million when he discovered the little fire insurance scam involving her father's thoroughbred racing stable.

"Why should I believe that you're not going to try and blackmail me again, Aaron?" she'd asked him.

"Darlin' child. It wasn't blackmail. You needed money. I needed money. It worked out for both of us."

She knew Aaron well enough to know that he wouldn't keep his word. The minute he had her in the nut-house he'd squeal to the cops. "After tonight, Aaron, you won't be telling anyone, anything."

She reached into the pocket of her Calvin Klein jeans and felt for the white cube of barbecue starter. "I'm not going to let you ruin my wedding, or the rest of my life, Aaron Cook."

She picked up the telephone and dialed his number. "Aaron. It's me," she told him when he answered. "I've been giving a lot of thought to what you said, and I agree. I can't get married with this hanging over my head. I'm on my way to your place now. I'll be there in twenty minutes and we'll take care of everything."

"I'm glad you're going to handle this," Aaron told her. "You'll feel much better in the morning."

"Yes, Aaron," she smiled into the receiver. "I'm sure that I'll feel much better in the morning. I'll see you in twenty minutes. Do you have any Jack Daniel's? Good, put some on ice for me. Dinner, no I can't stay for dinner. I have somewhere else to be."

Chapter Thirty Six

"I FEEL LIKE I'M in a fish bowl," Katherine commented to Ben as she gracefully descended the long carpeted staircase leading to the reception area of the main ballroom at the twenty-fifth firefighters awards night and gala. When they reached the last step, she took a deep breath and a firmer grip on Ben's arm. "I can't do this," she whispered.

"Yes you can, Kate," Ben whispered back. "You'll be fine. Go on."

"Okay, if you insist." Katherine left Ben on his own and wandered around the reception hall smiling and saying hello to faces she hadn't seen since Tom's funeral. She spoke with the chief, the battalion chiefs, and the district chiefs. She spoke to captains and lieutenants from across the city. Some faces were familiar to her and some she had never seen before.

"Hi, Katherine. How are you making out these days?" Fire Department Public Information Officer Mark Turner asked her.

"I'm doing well, Mark. Thank you for asking."

He took a deep breath and stood tall. "Katherine, I have something to tell you, and I really wish I didn't, but you're going to find out about it sooner or later, thanks to Jane Phillips."

Concern interrupted Katherine's smile. "What is it, Mark?"

He dropped his head and stared at the carpet. "Well, I just found out from my secretary..."

Katherine reached out and raised Mark's chin upward until his eyes met hers. "Mark, could you please look at me when you're talking to me."

"Sorry, Katherine," he blushed. "It's just that I don't know how to tell you this."

"Just tell me, Mark. It can't be that bad."

"Okay. As I was saying, I just spoke with my secretary and she advised me that tomorrow morning, Jane Phillips is running a piece on Tom's fire last month."

"That's natural," Katherine smiled. "She's a journalist."

"Well, there's something in that article that I think you should know about."

"And what might that be?"

"Well, at Tom's fire, the only reason he and his crew went into apartment 201 that night, even though they knew it wasn't safe, was because a woman told them that her kids were in apartment 201."

"What's so unusual about that, Mark? Firefighters always press on when they shouldn't, especially when there are children involved."

"That's just the thing, Katherine." Mark's face turned red. The kids weren't the lady's children. They were her cats." He readied his arms in case his news flash caused her to faint.

"I already know that, Mark," Katherine calmly told him.

"How do you know?"

"From Jane Phillips herself."

"She called you and told you about the article?"

"No. She called me the morning Tom died and wanted to come over to the house to do an interview. I told her it wasn't a good time. We did the interview the day after Tom's funeral."

Mark shook his head in frustration. The concern on his face turned to anger. "You know, just when I start to give that woman some credit, she blows it all to hell."

"Don't worry about it, Mark," Katherine smiled," and don't be so hard on her. Other than the fact that she doesn't have a sense of humor, she's actually quite a nice person. You should take the time to get to know her better. I think you'd like her."

"I have no use for that woman, and I'm going to put a stop to the article."

"Don't do that, Mark."

"And why not?"

"Because I think the article is a good thing. It shows people what our guys go through to save a life. Even when that life is a family pet."

"You ready to go in?" Ben asked as he walked into the conversation. "Hi, Mark, how are you?" The men exchanged a handshake.

"Fine, Ben, just fine." Mark gave Katherine a polite smile. "I better go find my seat. I'm sure we'll run into each other later."

"Shall we then?" Ben asked, offering Katherine his right arm.

"Shouldn't you be saving this arm for Rachel? Where is she by the way?" Katherine asked.

"She's not coming," Ben replied.

Katherine stopped dead in her tracks. "What do you mean she's not coming? I talked to her this morning and we were discussing what dress she was going to wear."

"She called me about five minutes ago. Apparently, something has gone sideways with her big real estate deal. You know the old factory down on the docks. The one her client wants to turn into a night club."

"Oh, I hope everything's okay. Rachel had her heart set on that deal." Katherine pulled Ben closer. "In fact, I'll let you in on a little secret."

"What's that?"

"Rachel told me if the deal went through, she was taking you to Tahiti for your honeymoon."

"That would be nice," Ben smiled. "I guess we better keep out fingers crossed."

"It's too bad she can't make it. I'm sure she would have had a wonderful time." Katherine offered Ben a silly grin. "It would have given you a chance to brush up on your dancing skills before the wedding."

"Let's get Billy married off first, then we'll worry about my wedding and my dancing skills, or lack there of." Ben let out a sigh as they walked to their table. "I can't wait till this year is over. It's been a rough one for a lot of us."

"I agree, but there's been some good come out of it too. You hooked up with Rachel and I am so happy for you, Ben." Katherine leaned over and gave him a peck on the cheek. "Now I'll have a sister-in-law!"

"It looks like you've got a daughter-in-law too," Ben smiled. "Billy has always looked at you like a surrogate mother. It seems that Sarah is doing the same thing. She's kept you pretty busy with wedding plans since Tom's funeral."

"Yes, she has, and I'm very grateful. It helps keep my mind off Tom and how much I miss him"

"Speaking of Sarah, she was at the hall the other night and Bruce happened to mention something about Michael's death. Well, she shot out of the room like a cannon. I had to get one of the female paramedics to convince her to come out of the head."

"Oh, I wouldn't worry about it." Katherine gave him a reassuring pat on the shoulder. "She's probably just having pre-wedding jitters. I'm sure that talking about Michael's death made her realize that she could lose Billy the same way."

When they reached their table, Katherine scanned the room in search of her daughter. "Ben, have you seen Samantha?"

"Yeah," he chuckled. "She met some hot little rookie. I think his name is Chad. She's warm for his form Katie. You better watch out or you'll end up a grandmother!"

She gave him a friendly slap on the shoulder, "Oh, Ben, stop that! Samantha is a responsible young woman and I'm not ready to be a grandmother."

"Do you want me to go find her?"

"Would you," she smiled.

"I'll be right back."

As Ben walked away Katherine couldn't help but notice the place card at the setting to her right. It had been reserved for her son Matthew. She was sure he'd come to terms with his father's death. They'd spoken several times since the funeral and each time he seemed much better. He'd even planned on attending tonight, but at the last minute he'd changed his mind. Matthew told her it was because of his upcoming exams, but

Katherine was sure there was another reason and she hoped that he would eventually tell her what it was.

In the meantime, she was thankful that Matthew had selected a career in law, not fire. She knew she couldn't go through losing another family member.

Chapter Thirty Seven

AS THE LAST DESSERT dish was removed from the table, tonight's master of ceremonies approached the podium. A hush fell over the crowd. "Good evening, ladies and gentlemen. For those of you who don't know me, my name is Marvin Gates. I hope everyone's enjoying themselves so far, and that you all got enough to eat." He put his hand over his eyes to block the glare of the lights, and peered towards the back of the room. "Especially our fine group of trainees at the back there, who are going to put on a ladder demonstration for all of us a little bit later." Hoots and hollers erupted from the table of recruits.

Katherine leaned over and whispered in her daughter's ear. "Which one is Chad?"

"I'll introduce you to him later," Samantha blushed.

"Ladies and gentlemen," Marvin continued. "I would like to thank each and every one of you for attending our twenty-fifth annual firefighters award night and gala. Especially, because this is the second one the ladies of our association have had to organize this year. Let's give them a round of applause."

When quiet returned to the room, Marvin offered his audience a proud smile. "Now, I have some good news for you. As you know the band that we hired to play at the gala when it was originally scheduled in June, couldn't be with us tonight." A rumble of disappointment spread through the crowd.

"That isn't good news, Marvin," someone yelled.

"I know you're all disappointed. Big Brass, has been playing this event for years." Marvin gave his audience a huge smile, "but they say a change is as good as a rest."

"So, who did you get, Marv? The department's pipe band?"

Marvin shook his head. "No, no we didn't. Our band may be one of the finest pipe bands around, but they aren't much on dance tunes!" A proud smile lit up the master of ceremonies' face. "Ladies and gentleman, I'm happy to say, this year, thanks to Ms. Jane Phillips, the fire department's newest friend, tonight's band will be none other than rock recording artists, Late Night Radio." The younger women in the crowd went wild, screaming and yelling out the name of the band.

Sarah leaned over and tapped Katherine on the shoulder. "How did Jane ever manage to get a band like that for the gala? I still can't believe it! They're huge recording stars!" The excitement rose in her voice. "Their latest album just went gold. The last time they were in town, Billy couldn't even get tickets to their concert. How did Jane manage to get them here? I thought they were on tour in Europe."

"Well, Sarah," Katherine chuckled, "the more I get to know Jane, the more I'm realizing how much pull her career in journalism has."

"That's the reason she got the band? Because of her pull in the newspaper industry?

"Actually, no. Jane happens to be a personal friend of the band. She went to school with Bobbie, the bass player. Speaking of Jane," Katherine looked across the table at the empty seat, "have you seen her?"

"Not since this afternoon, when she was here helping with the decorations. Come to think of it, I haven't seen her since Billy and I arrived."

"Maybe she's busy hunting down a story for tomorrow morning's paper. I heard sirens not too long ago. Perhaps she's out reporting on the fire."

"Ladies and gentleman! Ladies and gentleman!" Marvin tapped the podium to get his audience's attention. "We're running a little late and we have several awards to present here tonight, but before we get started with our presentation this evening, would everyone please stand in a minute of silence to pay honor to our six brothers who have fallen this year."

The room stood silently as Marvin read out their names. "Nozzle Man Dick Smyth, First Class Firefighter Nick Bond, Firefighter Michael Wells, Captain Tom Chambers, Nozzle Man Scott Tanaka and First Class Firefighter Gord Wheaton." When the minute of silence was over, the brass bell on the antique fire engine at the back of the room rang out six times. "Please be seated."

Katherine felt her legs tremble as she sat in her chair. Tears formed in the corners of her eyes but she refused to give into the temptation to cry. She'd cried enough.

Marvin cleared his throat. "Ladies and gentlemen, our first award this evening goes to a captain, and two of the firefighters we have just honored." He pulled his glasses and a piece of folded paper from the inside pocket of his dress uniform. He propped his glasses on his nose and carefully unfolded his notes. A hush fell over the audience.

"On New Year's Eve," Marvin began. "Fire Station No. 19 was the first hall dispatched to a building fire in the city's West End. When Captain Tom Chambers and his crew arrived at the scene, flames were visible on the second floor of the two-story walk-up apartment, and extending from the building onto the balcony. Also visible on the balcony, an elderly man and his pet dog – both in immediate danger of being surrounded by the fire.

"Recognizing the threatening situation, Firefighters Scott Tanaka and Gordon Wheaton immediately grabbed a ladder and raised it to the balcony to gain access. Once there, they discovered the elderly gentleman was paralyzed from the waist down and, therefore, unable to proceed down the ladder even with the assistance of the firefighters.

"Knowing that the balcony would soon be engulfed in flames, the crew acted quickly. Firefighters Tanaka and Wheaton, having been joined by Captain Chambers, unbuckled their duty coats and spread them over the gentleman and his pet to protect them from the intense heat, while the second-in crew quickly extinguished the flames.

"For their act of bravery, I'm proud to present this year's

Medal of Valor award to Captain Tom Chambers and the crew of No. 19."

When the applause died down Marvin continued. "I would now like to invite Mrs. Katherine Chambers up to the stage to accept the award on her husband's behalf."

When Marvin announced her name, Katherine turned to Ben with a horrified look on her face. "I can't do this Ben."

"Yes, you can." He squeezed her hand. "You'll be fine."

She turned to her daughter. "It's okay, Mom," Samantha grinned. "Go ahead. Uncle Ben's right. You'll be fine."

Katherine's palms were cold and clammy and her legs trembled as a member of the Honor Guard escorted her to the stage. When she stood at the podium, her heart pounded in her chest and she wished she could be anywhere but here. Everyone had fears and her biggest was public speaking. She could write a great letter to a local politician demanding action on an issue but when it came to standing up in front of a crowd, even now, she still froze.

Tom had been the driving force in getting Katherine to deal with her fears. He encouraged her to join Toast Masters and participating in the group helped her speak without stuttering or stammering as she had done when she was a child.

Katherine discovered over the years that what had helped her the most, was always having Tom in the room. He hadn't missed one of her speeches in the past three years and just knowing that he was present always calmed her nerves and gave her confidence.

Like a baseball coach and his player, Tom had signs and signals that told Katherine when to speed up and when to slow down. When to throw a curve ball, or pull in the outfield. When he patted the top of his head, it was a signal that her speech had just hit a grand slam home run.

Tonight, Katherine would have no manager, no signals from the dugout. She was on her own and she would be on her own for the rest of her life. Tears formed in the corners of her eyes and she fought hard to hold them back.

Tom had been so looking forward to this evening, she

thought. He'd prepared a speech and polished the brass buttons on his dress uniform. He was anxious to tell his crew, in front of all these people, how proud he was to call himself their Captain.

I'll get through this evening if it kills me, Katherine reassured herself as she stared out at the sea of faces in front of her. She took a deep breath and offered her audience a warm smile. "Good evening, ladies and gentlemen," she began. "First of all, on behalf of myself, and my family, I would like to take this opportunity to thank the women of Helping Hands and all of the members of the Fire Department who have provided their support to all of the firefighters families during this most difficult year."

Out of habit, Katherine looked over the heads of the crowd towards the back of the room expecting to see Tom standing there, but he wasn't. He would never be standing there again. A brief moment of anxiety swept through her body and her knees started to shake. "Tonight, I've been asked to say a few words on behalf of my late husband. A word about the courageous men of Fire Hall No. 19's 'D' Platoon. Not all of those men are here tonight, but they will remain in our hearts forever.

"Tom was thrilled when he learned that his crew was being honored with this award. In fact, he worked on his speech for weeks finding just the perfect words to express how proud he was of each and every one of his crewmembers.

"I asked if I could read his speech, and he told me that I couldn't see it until it was finished. Then he hid it. I found the speech when I was going through his things. I'm not going to read it to you in its entirety, because it would take a month of Sundays. We all know how long winded my husband was." A wave of laughter erupted through the crowd.

"I would, however, like to share a few words from that speech with the three remaining members of my husband's crew, and with the wives of Scott Tanaka and Gord Wheaton. They are words that I know Tom would have wanted you all to hear."

Katherine focused her attention on the table where the three men sat with their wives and the wives of their fallen comrades and smiled warmly. "Brian, you were Tom's lieutenant, his second in command. He often told me that you had a knack for detail, like none he had ever seen. He knew that someday you would make an excellent captain. Congratulations on your promotion."

Brian offered her a sad smile of acknowledgement. He was glad for the promotion, he just wished it would have been under different circumstances.

Katherine turned her attention to Wendy Wheaton and Ted Brown. "Many a dinner conversation at our house consisted of Tom ranting on, and on, about the hair raising ride he'd gotten from Gord, or you Ted, but I'll let you in on a little secret. Tom would have put the two of you up against any driving team in the city. In his eyes, you and Gord were the best rig operators around."

Next, Katherine smiled at Sandra Tanaka. "Sandra, I can't tell you how many times Tom told me that he not only had the best nozzle man in the city, he had the best cook too!" The Japanese woman offered her a bow of thanks.

Katherine turned to Ted Brown and offered Tom's junior man a motherly smile. "Ted, I know that you weren't part of Tom's crew, on the night they are being honored for, but you were part of his crew for a short time, and he spoke very highly of you. If he were here right now, the first thing he'd probably do, is congratulate you for all of the practical jokes you put up with. We all know that to work with Tom, you had to have a sense of humor. If Tom were here now, he'd thank you for your contribution to this year's 'Fire Watch' lottery." The people in the room who understood the joke laughed hysterically and broke into applause.

Ted stood up from the table, his face red with embarrassment. "Thank you. Thank you very much." He bowed to the audience. "It was my pleasure."

Katherine looked back at her audience. "Tom loved being

a firefighter. He loved doing what he did for a living. He knew when he joined the department that the job came with risks.

"Tom, Scott and Gord died doing their job, and every firefighter in this room would have done the same thing. So, tonight, on this joyous occasion when we are here to celebrate accomplishments, and bravery, don't weep for Tom. He wouldn't have wanted that."

Katherine raised her glass into the air. "Ladies and gentlemen on behalf of my late husband and his crew, I graciously accept this award. It will be proudly display at Fire Hall No. 19."

Chapter Thirty Eight

WITH BLACK PUMPS IN hand, Rachel raced through the lobby of the Fairmount Olympia Hotel. She had hoped to make it to the gala before Katherine accepted Tom's award, but by the look of the No. 1 dress uniforms mulling about the lobby, she was sure she'd missed the presentation.

At the top of the staircase leading to the ballroom, she wished for a moment that she could slide down the banister like she'd done as a child in her grandmother's house. It would be much faster, but highly inappropriate.

When Rachel reached the bottom of the staircase, she turned right. She'd taken no more than three steps when she ran smack dab into Heather Kennedy. "Oh, my God. Heather, I'm so sorry," Rachel apologized. She took a step backward stared down at Heather's dress. It was soaked. "Look what I've done!"

"Don't worry about it, Rachel," Heather smiled as she brushed the ice cubes and Pepsi from the front of her gown. "It will be fine."

"It most certainly won't be fine," Rachel told her. "We have to get that out right away or it will stain." She took Heather by the arm. "Come on, we'll go to the powder room. I always carry Perrier in my purse for just such an emergency."

Rachel pulled Heather down the hall and through the double doors into the ladies washroom. "Now, take that off and I'll have the stain out of it in a flash."

Heather unzipped her high collar, long sleeve dress and as if fell from her body, a gasp escaped from Rachel's throat.

"What's wrong?" Heather asked as she climbed out of the garment.

"I'm sorry, please forgive me. I don't mean to stare."

"Oh," Heather grinned. "My battle wounds." She reached up and ran her hands across her chest. "Don't worry about it. I'm used to the scars, but they do have a tendency to flip out people who've never seen them."

"Here, give me that." Rachel took the garment from Heather and covered the stain with sparkling water. "This will just take a minute." She gently rubbed the material and handed it back. "That's better. Now hold it under the dryer. In five minutes, it will be as good as new."

"Oh, my God. What happened to you," Sarah asked as she walked out of a bathroom stall.

"Rachel and I had a collision," Heather chuckled.

"No, not the dress. Your arms and chest."

"Sarah," Rachel scolded, "that's not a very polite question."

"No, it's okay," Heather blushed. "I don't mind talking about it. In fact, years ago my shrink told me that it was good to talk about it." Heather held her dress to the hand dryer and hit the button. "I got these when I was a rookie on the Chicago Fire Department."

"What happened?"

"We were called to an apartment fire. It was an apartment that a buddy of mine lived in. By the time we arrived on scene, there were flames shooting out of every window in his corner suite apartment."

"I know a little about Chicago," Jane Phillips interrupted as she walked into the powder room and the conversation.

"Where have you been?" Sarah asked. "You promised the graduating class that you'd introduce them to the guys in the band. They've been driving me nuts and ..." Sarah stopped in mid sentence and looked at the front of Jane's outfit. "What did you do to your blouse? Is that soot?" She reached up to touch the stain but Jane slapped her hand away.

"No, it's grease. I had a flat. Go on, Heather, finish your story," Jane encouraged.

"I jumped off the rig," Heather continued, "grabbed my gear and followed my lieutenant into the apartment building. As we headed towards the elevator, he told us that he was going to set up the staging area on the ninth floor."

"What's a staging area?" Sarah asked.

"It's the place where they set up command inside of the building," Rachel answered.

Jane raised a questioning brow. "You seem to know a lot about fires Rachel."

"I've been studying," she smiled. "I'm on the department's new public awareness committee. I have to know this stuff."

"Well, to make a long story shorter," Heather continued, "my lieutenant ordered my partner, Bernie Peterson, and myself to go up to the top floor and search for occupants as we made our way back down to the staging area. On the sixteenth floor, there was a haze of smoke in the air. When I pulled down my facemask, Bernie asked me if I was afraid of a little smoke."

"What an asshole," Jane commented as she applied fresh eye shadow to her lids.

"Anyway, we started checking apartment doors to see if they were hot and if anyone was inside. Halfway down the hall a frightened Asian woman opened her door. Bernie handed her off to me and told me to take her down a flight and show her how to get out.

"Well, the poor woman was scared to death. I knew I couldn't just take her down a flight and expect her to get out by herself. There was a fire burning on eleven. I decided I'd take her down to the staging area. Someone there could help her out of the building."

"So, how did you get burned?" Sarah asked.

"Well," Heather began again. "When I got back to where I'd left Bernie, he was sitting on the floor in front of an apartment half way down the hall. His arms were folded across his lap and his chin hung to his chest. I raced toward him afraid something was wrong. When I asked him if he was okay, he unfolded his arms, tipped up the front of his fire helmet like a cowboy tips up a Stetson and told me he was just taking a break.

He let out a grunt, pulled himself up off the floor and rolled the top of his glove back into place. Then, he told me that we may have something. He said the door he was standing in front of was hot."

"What did he do next." Rachel asked.

"I'll tell you what he did. He took a step backwards, kicked his right leg out in front of him, and planted his size twelve-rubber boot in the middle of the door. When it swung open, black smoke billowed into the hallway."

"Did he contact the rest of the crew?" Sarah inquired.

"Oh, yeah. He radioed the sector officer and told him we had something burning."

"Then what happened?"

Heather roller her eyes. "Well, Bernie never did like me. When we first met at training I thought he was okay, but after working with him for a month, I changed my mind."

"Why?"

"He didn't like women on the fire department. He mentioned constantly that the city spent a fortune to get us on the job and after a year, most of us had transferred from the fire floor, or were off on MAT leave."

"So, how did you get burned?" Sarah asked again.

Jane gave her a strange look. "You seem to be awful interested in how the poor girl got burned. Is there something you're not telling us? There have been a lot of fires in the city lately. Had anything to do with them?"

"Jane, give her a break," Rachel remarked. "She's just curious. Sarah is about to marry a firefighter. Something like this could happen to Billy. Go on, Heather, finish your story."

"Well, Bernie told me that if I thought I was such a shit-hot firefighter I could go in first. I couldn't believe my ears. I'd been taught in training to always stay with my senior guy. I'd also been taught to stay behind him. It wasn't my responsibility to go in first. It was his. I told him he was nuts, that neither one of us should be going in. We didn't have a hose line and from the amount of smoke billowing into the hall, I could tell that we needed one.

"Bernie told me to quit being such a baby and ordered me inside to look for casualties. I pulled my facemask into place, turned on my air cylinder and got down on my hands and knees. My legs were shaking like a leaf when I crawled across the threshold into the thick, black, smoke. Ten feet into the room, I stopped and looked over my shoulder expecting Bernie to be right behind me. Much to my surprise, he wasn't. I was alone."

"Figures," Jane piped up. "Men are all the same. They make you take the heat."

"I knew I shouldn't be there by herself," Heather continued. "It was hot, and smoky, and I didn't have water in case I came face to face with the flames. I turned around and headed back in the direction I thought I'd come from. I couldn't see more than a foot in front of me, and I was wishing I had a hose line to follow back. I'd learned in training that in a situation like this, the big coupling would take me back to the big truck.

"It was getting hotter than hell. I could feel the skin under my T-shirt and bicycle shorts starting to burn from the heat of my own perspiration. My father always told me that I should wear long johns and a long sleeve T-shirt under my duty gear. He told me the long johns help absorb the sweat and keep you from boiling like a lobster in a pot. Right about then, I was wishing I'd have listened."

"You didn't get your burns from that, did you?" Jane asked.

"No, not from that," Heather told her. Anyway, I'd traveled no more than three feet when I heard something that sounded like a baby crying. I stopped, and listened. When I heard it again, I turned left and crawled forward towards the sound.

"I'd gone no more than three feet when something hit my left shoulder and stopped me in my tracks. I moved my hands along the base and sides of the object, figuring out that it was a wall unit. I positioned myself in front of the obstacle and slowly stood up. When I found a knob, I pulled the door open towards me. The cat that jumped from the top shelf scared the hell out of me. I fell over backward and pulled the furniture down on top of me."

Rachel raised her hands to her mouth. "Heather that's terrible. How did you get out? Did that Bernie person come in to help you?"

"No!" Heather exclaimed. "Apparently, he stayed out in the hall."

"Then how did you get out?" Jane asked.

"Two of the guys from another fire hall pulled me out."

"Was anyone else injured in the fire?" Sarah asked.

"Not in that fire," Heather told her, "but in a fire in the same building."

Sarah shook her head. "I don't understand?"

"My buddy, Travis Greenwood, a guy that I went through training with died that night."

Jane turned from her reflection in the mirror and looked at Heather. "But I thought you said that there were no other firefighters injured."

"Travis wasn't on shift the night. There were two fires burning in the same building at the same time. The one I was injured in, and the original fire that started in Travis's apartment. Travis died in bed."

Sarah felt the blood drain from her face and the room started to spin. "I think I'm going to be sick." She put her hand over her mouth and raced into an empty cubicle.

"What's up with her," Jane asked as she applied a fresh coat of lipstick.

"Maybe she's had too much to drink," Heather replied.

"Well, I'm out of here." Jane tossed the bright red lipstick back in her purse. "Time to meet my awaiting public." With that, she was gone.

"Heather, again, I'm so sorry about your dress," Rachel apologized. "Please, let me pay for the dry cleaning."

"Oh, don't worry about it." She pulled the garment from under the hand dryer. "See, you can't even tell."

"Sorry about that girls," Sarah moaned as she opened the stall door. "I don't know what came over me."

Rachel took her by the arm and helped her to the sink. "Are you going to be okay?"

"Yes, thank you. If you could just wait a minute and then help me back to the table, I would sure appreciate it."

"Oh, there goes my pager." Heather reached into her purse and pulled out the small, black object. "The district chief," she remarked as she looked down at the number. "There must have been a fire somewhere."

Heather dropped the pager back in her purse and gave Sarah and Rachel a disappointed look. "Well, I guess my evening is over. Duty calls. Have a good night ladies." With that Heather turned on her heels and headed out the door.

Chapter Thirty Nine

RACHEL HELPED SARAH TO a chair in the banquet hall then sat down beside Ben. "Sorry it took me so long to get here," she apologized as she leaned over and gave Ben a peck on the cheek.

A pleased smile lit up his face. "I wasn't expecting to see you tonight. When I hadn't heard from you by ten, I figured you weren't going to make it."

"I've been here for awhile actually."

"What have you been doing? Checking out the single firefighters?"

"I'm not interested in single firefighters anymore," Rachel laughed. "I'm only interested in the firefighter I'm going to marry." She took his face in her hands and slid her moist tongue into his mouth.

"You better quit that," Ben moaned, "or we'll be going home earlier than planned.

"That suits me just fine," she winked.

"So, where were you?" He asked

"When?"

"Just now. Before you came to the table?"

Rachel's heart beat faster. "I ran into Heather Kennedy in lobby."

"Did you have a nice chat?"

"No, Ben," she blushed. "I literally ran into her. Spilt her drink all over the front of her dress. I felt like such an idiot. Did you know that she was burned in a fire when she was just a rookie?'

"Yes. As a matter of fact, her dad uses it in his training lectures." Ben put his arm around Rachel and pulled her closer. "How did your meeting go?"

"I'm not so sure," she frowned.

"Is your guy still going to buy the place?"

"I don't know that either. It may be coming off the market."

"I thought the owner was anxious to sell."

"Apparently he was, but his brother-in-law told him he'd get more cash from burning the place down. Do you believe that? Why would someone make a stupid comment like that? Doesn't he know that arson is a criminal offence."

"It may be a criminal offence," Ben agreed, "but it's one of the hardest things to prove."

"Excuse me people," Marvin announced from the stage. "It's time to present the winners of the fire watch lottery with their prizes."

Rachel looked at Ben in confusion. "The fire watch lottery. What's he talking about?"

"Well, in fire halls all across the city, when we get a new class of recruits, we scout them out like horses on a racing form. Do you know anything about race horses and racing forms?" Ben asked.

"A little bit," Rachel smiled.

"Well, on a racing form, it tells you about the horse's previous experience. So, we check with the training staff to see if the new recruit fell for any pranks during training. Next, like a horse, we see how many races they have won."

"How many races they've won? I don't understand."

"What I mean is, we check to see if they have ever been on the fire floor. You know have they got any experience. Would they know that we love to play practical jokes on our probies. Then we check their age." Ben gave Rachel a devious grin. "The younger the rookie, the more gullible they appear to be. Last, but not least, we find out whose hall they will be going to. Who their captain and crew will be."

Rachel shook her head. "I'm confused. I don't understand what any of this has to do with the lottery?"

"Well, Rachel, how it works," Bruce began, "on the rookie's first day on the hall, we tell him that throughout his first month, he'll be asked to do specific tasks. Some of them may seem strange, but it's not his place to ask questions.

"We tell them, for each task they complete, they get a gold star. If, by the end of the second month, they have collected all fifteen gold stars, they'll be given the honor of taking fire watch. No, rookie ever gets all fifteen stars."

"Then what's the point, Bruce?" Rachel asked.

"Well, on a rookie's last night shift of their second month on the job, during dinner, the nozzle man points out the fact that the probie didn't get all the stars required to be the shifts fire watch officer. Of course, the kid starts to mope," Bruce added, "so the lieutenant suggests that the crew take a vote and decide if they should give him the honor anyway."

"And of course, everyone votes yes, right?" Rachel grinned.

"You're catching on," Bruce winked. "The captain tells the rookie to meet him in the office at 23:00 hours dressed in full firefighter turnout gear. Boots, hitch, duty coat and helmet.

When they show up, eager and anxious to perform their duties, they're taken outside, where they're given a lawn chair, a flashlight, a bell and a district map for the area. Then, the rookie is ordered to climb up the ladder to the roof. For the next twelve hours, the rookie's job will be to watch for fires."

Rachel shook her head. "Do you mean to tell me that you have guys who actually stay up there all night?" She laughed.

"Most of them figure it out after an hour or so," Ben grinned, "but we had one kid who was on the roof all night. Bruce, do you remember Charlie Beck at No. 6?"

"Oh, yeah," Bruce laughed. "He was the rookie who started about four years ago. The night they set him up for fire watch, at about two in the morning, there was actually a fire. The kid started ringing the bell like a mad man. The guys in the hall ignored it of course. They were sure the kid figured it was all a big joke and wanted to see if he could get the crew outside.

They changed their tune when the tones started going off inside the hall."

"And, what happened to Charlie Beck?" Rachel asked. "Did he go to the call?"

"Hell, no!" Bruce laughed. "The guys took off and left him on the roof. He was there until the crew got back at six in the morning."

"Excuse me. Excuse me ladies and gentlemen." Marvin Gates tapped on the microphone. "It's almost midnight and before the band begins its last set of the evening, I would like to make the draw for our fire watch lottery. So dig into your pockets and pull out your tickets.

"Now, can I get probationary firefighters, Todd Williams, Barry Evans and Ted Brown to join me." The crowd erupted in applause as the three gentlemen made their way to center stage. When they were standing by Marvin's side, he pulled seven envelopes from his inside pocket. "Ladies and gentlemen," Marvin began, "in third place, Probationary Firefighter Ted Brown with a time of thirty-one minutes and eight seconds. Ted, would you please step forward and accept your check in the amount of three hundred dollars."

Marvin handed the young man an envelope and turned back to his audience. "Now, we all know that Ted is going to give his cash back to the Children's Hospital. Aren't you Ted?" The young man blushed and handed the envelope back to Martin. "Congratulations, Ted, you've supported a good cause." The audience applauded the firefigher's generosity as he left the stage.

"Now, the person who predicted the closest time to Ted's," Marvin continued, "is Paul Caster with a time of thirty minutes." Marvin held his hand over his brow to block the glare of the lights. "Is Paul here?" He asked.

"Right here," the firefighter yelled from the back of the banquet hall.

"You can collect your three hundred dollars at the union hall on Monday, Paul."

Marvin presented checks in the amount of five hundred

dollars to Probationary Firefighter Barry Evans, and the man who bet on him, Firefighter Gus Patterson. The final two checks, totaling one thousand dollars each, were presented to Probationary Firefighter Todd Williams and his counterpart District Chief Garry Hampton. Like his colleagues, Todd turned his check back into Marvin in support of the Children's Hospital.

"These three fine firefighters have just contributed fifteen hundred dollars to the Children's Hospital," Marvin commented. "Let's give them a big round of applause."

When the crowd settled down, Marvin reached into his pocket and pulled out the seventh envelope. "Here it is people, the balance of monies raised after paying off the winners." He turned to the band's drummer.

"Ladies and gentlemen, here it is." Marvin ripped open the envelope and pulled out the check. "It's official ladies and gentlemen, we've beat last year's total. This year on behalf of Captain Tom Chambers, the man who created the fire watch lottery, we are happy to donate ten thousand, and fifty dollars to the Children's Hospital."

"Tom would be proud," Katherine smiled, "and on that happy note, I think I'm going to take my weary body home. I'll see everyone at the airport next Friday." She leaned over and gave Sarah a peck on the cheek. "Now, you get some sleep tonight dear and quit worrying about your wedding. Rachel has everything under control."

"Yes, I do," Rachel smiled. "I spoke with the wedding coordinator at the Fairmount Banff Springs Hotel this afternoon and she has assured me that your wedding will be perfect."

Excitement rose in Sarah's voice. "Rachel, I still can't believe that Billy and I are getting married in the heart of the Canadian Rockies on Christmas Eve! When I was a child my father always told me that someday I'd have a fairytale wedding."

"Well, your father was right Sarah," Rachel smiled. "Yours will be a fairy tale wedding. I promise."

Chapter Forty

December 23rd

THE PRESIDENTIAL SUITE AT the Fairmount Banff Springs Hotel in Banff, Alberta, Canada was magnificent. The one thousand square foot unit with its three hundred and sixty-degree view of the Spray and Bow River Valleys, offered unsurpassed luxury.

The split-level living room boasted a wood-burning fireplace, a grand piano and a library. There was a guest bathroom and a pantry. In the master bedroom there was a king-size canopy bed. The ensuite bathroom, with its whirlpool and shower, was finished in marble.

"So, Captain." Tony gave Ben a friendly slap on the shoulder. "It looks like you're marrying into money! Billy told me that Rachel is picking up the tab for his and Sarah's entire wedding. The private jet to fly all of us up here. The limos that got us here from the airport, this party, tomorrow's wedding dinner, and Garth told me that she's even picking up the tab for our hotel rooms."

"Yeah, pretty amazing isn't it," Ben mumbled as he watched his bride-to-be float around the room like a butterfly, stopping at each guest and chatting only long enough to make them feel comfortable before moving on to the next.

Tony folded his arms across his chest. "What I'd like to know, is how she pulled it off?"

"She's quite the little hostess, isn't she," Ben smiled proudly.

"I'm not talking about her charm, boss. I'm taking about her pull." Tony winked.

"Pardon me?"

"Money aside, Captain, we all know she's got more cash than God, how did she pull it off? How did she manage to book a classy place like this when tomorrow is Christmas Eve?

"There's tons of snow in the mountains and I understand that the ski resorts around here are anticipating a record year. I'm sure that's the reason for all of the no vacancy signs I saw when we were driving up Main Street. So," Tony gave Ben a nudge, "how did she pull it off? How did she manage to get this place? Does she have connections or something?"

Ben shrugged his shoulders. "Well, I guess so. Her father was a big wheel with the Canadian Pacific Railroad. At one time, the railroad owned this hotel. Rachel still knows a lot of people in the business."

"Well, it's quite the joint," Tony smiled. "Maybe she can do the same thing for me."

"Do the same thing for you?" Ben gave him a baffled look. "What are you talking about, Tony?"

"I'm getting married too!"

"You're what?" Ben exclaimed.

"I'm getting married too." The excitement rose in his voice. "Maybe Rachel can do the same thing for me!"

"Wait a minute." Ben gave his head a shake. "Did I hear you right? Did you just say that you were getting married?"

"I sure did!" Tony beamed.

Ben held his hands to his chest. "Quick," he yelled over the hum of conversation. "Call 911. I'm having a heart attack! Our confirmed bachelor is getting married." The room fell to a stunned silence.

"Ladies and gentleman, I've just been informed that No. 5's confirmed bachelor, First Class Firefighter Tony DeMonte, is going to tie the knot." Ben looked around the room at he members of his crew. "I didn't even know he was seeing someone. Did you know Pete?"

The lieutenant shook his head. "No."

"What about you, Garth? Did you know anything about this?"

"Sure didn't, Captain," Garth answered back.

"No one knew," Tony grinned. "In fact, I didn't know myself until a few weeks ago. It's been kind of a whirlwind romance."

"So, don't keep us in suspense," Bruce shouted from the other side of the living room. "Who's the unfortunate bride-to-be?"

Tony's face turned beet red and he nervously kicked the carpet with the toe of his shoe. "You're never going to believe this," he began, "but..."

"I am." Jane Phillips announced as she made her grand entrance into Sarah and Billy's wedding rehearsal party. "I'm the blushing bride." Jane tossed her head and strolled across the room like a runway model; one foot gracefully moving in front of the other. Her shapely hips swaying from side to side.

"How do you like my engagement ring?" Jane stuck her hand in Rachel's face. "Isn't it great! Tony's fire department ring. I'm borrowing it," she snickered, "until we can pick out a diamond. Then, my collection will be complete!" Jane raised her right hand to her neck and felt for the gold chain that rested just below the collar of her turtleneck.

"Your collection?" Rachel asked.

"Yes, you know, the something old, something new, something borrowed and something blue thing that every bride is to have on her person when she walks down the isle."

"Jane," Bruce yelled from the back of the room. "What on earth does a gorgeous creature like you see in a skinny kid like him?"

"It must be my charming personality," Tony blushed.

Alice Bradley leaned over and poked her husband in the ribs. "Bruce, that woman goes through firefighters like socks. Didn't she go out with Ben at one time? And then there was Michael Wells. Now it's Tony."

"Might as well keep it in the family dear," he laughed. "Maybe she'll pick me next!"

"Not likely," Alice groaned.

"Oh, come on, honey. Who could resist this body?" Bruce grabbed the spare tire around his waist and gave it a shake.

"Ladies and gentleman," Ben raised his crystal champagne flute into the air. "This calls for a toast. To Tony and Jane."

"Here, here. To Tony and Jane," the crew of No. 5 and their wives replied.

"When's the wedding?" Someone asked.

"We haven't decided yet," Tony answered, "but if you're not busy Rachel, how about taking care of ours too?"

Rachel looked over at Ben and smiled. "I'm going to be busy planning my own wedding, but thanks for asking."

Tony shook his head. "Well, it's going to take a lot to top this one."

"Excuse me, Mr. Taylor," the butler interrupted, "there's an RCMP officer outside to see you sir. Will you come with me please."

"Sure." Ben handed Billy his drink. "Here, hold this for me. I'll be right back."

"Billy, will you excuse me too, please."

He turned and looked at his fiancé. "Yeah, Sarah. Are you okay?"

"I just have a bit of a headache," she answered in a whisper. "I'm going to go take a pill."

Sarah made her way to the master bedroom and opened her purse. Her hands shook as she rummaged through the contents in search of the tranquilizers. "Maybe one of these will calm me down." She snapped off the cap, took out a pill and popped it in her mouth.

She'd been stressed for weeks but it wasn't because of her wedding, it was because of the visit she'd gotten from Heather Kennedy.

A week after the gala, Heather showed up unannounced. She wanted to ask some questions about Michael Wells. She was investigating the circumstances surrounding his death.

Sarah told Heather that she met Michael for the first time when Billy introduced them at Fire Hall No.5, but she was sure the arson investigator hadn't believed her. Now, the Canadian cops were here to talk to Ben and she couldn't help but wonder if there was a connection.

Sarah slowly walked to the window. Outside, the mountains and valleys were covered in a blanket of white. Snowflakes fell from the sky like diamonds. She couldn't believe she was actually here, in this hotel, about to marry the man of her dreams in a wedding fit for a princess. Her father would be proud.

For a brief moment, a smile danced across Sarah's face. It faded, when she realized that everything could change. What if she had killed Michael? What would happen then? Would Billy still come and visit her in prison? Maybe she could share a cell with Janis Johnson.

"It's pretty amazing isn't it?"

Sarah jumped at the sound of Billy's voice. She grabbed her chest and spun around to face him. "You scared me!"

"Sorry, I didn't mean to. I just wanted to see if the pill helped?"

"Yes, thank you. It did."

Billy walked to where Sarah was standing and put his arm around her waist. "It's amazing how there can be a full moon in the sky, and it can still be snowing. Only in Canada, eh!" He gave her a kiss on the forehead. "Some of the guys and their wives are leaving. You want to come and say goodnight?"

Sarah shook her head. "Would you mind if I didn't? I'm sure everyone will understand."

"Not a problem," he smiled. "I'll tell them they can see you tomorrow night at 20:01, when you walk down the isle."

Sarah stood on her tiptoes and gave Billy a kiss. "Thank you."

"There you are, Billy," Rachel called out from the doorway. "I've been looking all over for you."

"Hi, Rachel. What's up?"

"Ben wants to see you. He's in the library on a conference call with Heather Kennedy."

Sarah felt the blood drain from her face and her knees started to shake. Heather Kennedy was on the phone. She was talking to Ben. Ben wanted to talk to Billy. Her soon-to-be perfect life was about to blow up in her face.

"Sure thing, Rachel." He turned to his bride. "I'll be back in a minute. Don't go away."

As Billy walked passed Rachel, he leaned over and whispered in her ear. "See if there's something bothering Sarah, will you. She's really jumpy."

"I will," Rachel whispered back.

When Billy was gone, Rachel walked across the room and stood behind Sarah. "It's beautiful here, isn't it?"

"Yes, it is," Sarah replied as she stared out the window. She took a deep breath and let out a long sigh. "I went to Austria with my father for Christmas, the year my mother died. There was lots of snow, but I don't remember it being as beautiful as this."

For a long while, the two women stood and stared out the window at the picture postcard view. Sarah broke the silence. "Rachel, what happens if this doesn't work?"

"If what doesn't work?"

"If this marriage doesn't work. What happens if Billy learns something about me that he can't live with, and he decides to leave me."

"What did you do?" Rachel laughed. "Kill someone?"

Sarah's body shook. Her face turned red. "Don't joke about something like that," she blurted out. "That's not funny!"

"Sarah, what's wrong with you?" Rachel reached out and took her by the shoulders to steady her. "Why are you getting so upset?"

"What if I did kill someone Rachel? Do you think Billy would stay with me?"

Rachel gave the girl a puzzled look. "You're not making any sense. Maybe you should sit down."

Rachel led Sarah to the bed. "Sit," she gave a gentle nudge. "I'll get you a glass of water and something to calm your nerves."

Sarah's hands sook as she accepted the cool, clear liquid. "Thank you," she whispered.

"You've had a pretty busy day. I think all you need is a good night's sleep. Here, this will help." Rachel opened her handbag and took out a small brown bottle of pills. "One of these, and you'll sleep like a baby," she smiled.

"What is it?" Sarah asked as she accepted the little yellow tablet.

"Valium."

"What are you doing with Valium? You're the calmest person I know."

"I use it when I can't sleep. Go on, take it," Rachel encouraged.

Sarah gave her an appreciative smile. "Maybe I'll just keep it for later, when I really need it."

Chapter Forty One

BEN SHOT UP IN bed, his hair and body soaked with perspiration.

"Ben, what's wrong?" Rachel asked as she reached up and touched him on the shoulder. "Are you okay?"

"It's nothing. I just need some air. Go back to sleep."

"Okay, "Rachel yawned as she drew the duvet back over her head.

Ben slid from under the satin sheets and closed the door behind him as he stepped out of the room. He grabbed a bottle of Scotch on his way to the library and plopped himself down in the leather chair behind the desk. He unscrewed the cap from the bottle, and took two big gulps.

"I can't believe this is happening." Ben clutched the bottle to his chest and leaned back in the chair. He closed his eyes, and forced his mind to recall every detail of the telephone conversation he'd had earlier with Heather Kennedy.

***

"Ben, do you remember me telling you in Michael's hospital room, a week or so after the fire, that I thought Brandon's Furniture Store had been booby trapped to get a firefighter? Well, now I believe it was one specific firefighter. Michael Wells himself!

"I've been digging into his past and I've uncovered some very interesting skeletons. He was involved in an arson slash, murder case years ago that took the life of a prominent Kentucky resident. The wife was convicted of both charges, but only after Michael Wells sang to the cops.

"He'd been living at the estate, posing as the wife's, stepbrother. Apparently, the only relationship between Michael and this Janis Johnson person was a physical one.

"She just got out on parole. At first, I thought that maybe she'd tracked Michael down, and was out to get her revenge, but that didn't play right. She only got out a week before the fire and she would have had to know what city Michael was in, what hall he was stationed at and what shift he was on. I thought she might have had someone on the inside working for her, but I checked with the warden and the woman was pretty much a loaner, so that took her off my suspect board.

"Jack Crawford, the man who died had a young daughter. Her name was Sarah. After his death, the child was shipped off to live with relatives. I've talked to some of them, weird bunch. They all told me that they lost contact with her years ago. No one knows where she is. She just vanished off the face of the earth.

"But here's something interesting. One of the relatives gave me a picture of the kid. I had the boys at the police lab add a few years and what they gave back to me was a picture of Sarah Baker, Billy's soon to be bride."

***

Chapter Forty Two

IT WAS 7:30 CHRISTMAS Eve. Sarah Baker and Billy Simpson were scheduled to be married, in half an hour. Heather Kennedy and Seattle Homicide Detective, Dick Dickerson, were about to change that.

"Her old man must have cash," Dickerson commented as the black unmarked RCMP police car pulled up in front of the hotel.

When the vehicle came to a stop, Heather got out and slammed the door. "Sarah doesn't have a father."

Dick glared across the hood of the car. "Is there something bothering you, Kennedy?" He asked.

You're damn right there's something bothering me, she told herself as she marched around the vehicle and stood toe to toe with him. "And you know exactly what it is, Dick!" Since they'd landed at the Calgary International Airport, two and a half-hours ago, Heather had been trying to convince Dick to hold off on the arrest until tomorrow but he refused. Some days she really hated her job.

"Are you ready to go?" He asked as he reached inside his trench coat and felt for the cold metal revolver that rested under his left arm.

"No, I'm not ready to go!" Heather grabbed the lapels of his trench coat and gave him a shake. "Dick, can you just not be such a Dick for a minute! Can't you, just for once, stop and smell the roses?"

She let go of his coat and took a step back. "Take a look around you. Have you ever seen a more perfect setting for a

Christmas Eve wedding? This beautiful old hotel nestled in the mountains. A midnight blue sky filled with stars. The moon dancing off the white snow." Heather took a deep breath and inhaled the cold night air into her lungs. "Can't you smell that?"

"Smell what?"

"Fresh air Dick! Clean, fresh, mountain air. Come on take a whiff." She gave him a friendly poke in the chest. "Just one, deep, whiff. You'll feel better."

"I don't have time for this Heather. I have a job to do."

"Oh, come on." She offered him her best smile. "Just one deep breath. That's all I ask. Besides, I gave you my cashews on the plane."

The detective rolled his eyes and shook his head. "All right, if you insist, just one. Then can we go arrest the woman?"

"Yes, Dick, then we can go arrest the woman."

Dickerson took one quick deep breath and exhaled. "There, are you happy now?"

"Oh, come on, Dick," Heather frowned, "you can do better than that. I mean a deep breath. You know, the one that comes right from the bottom of your lungs."

"Fine, if it will make you happy, I'll take a deep breath.

Heather watched as Dick sucked the crisp night air into his lungs. When he exhaled, she could almost see the tension leave his body. "There, doesn't that feel better?" She asked.

"Yes, I must admit, it does." He straightened the lapels of his coat. "Now, let's go make the arrest."

As he turned to walk away, she pulled at his sleeve. "It's Christmas Eve, Dick, and there's a wedding about to take place. Can't we wait and do this in the morning?" She begged.

"The wedding isn't taking place for half an hour, now lets go."

Reluctantly, Heather followed Detective Dickerson and the RCMP officer up the stairs and into the main lobby of the hotel. Just inside the front door, she spotted Ben talking to Billy. She reached forward and touched Dick's shoulder. "Ben's over there. I better go tell him what's happening. We were cut off last night during our phone conversation."

"Fine," Dick commented over his shoulder. "Don't be long. I'm going to find the bride's room."

Heather made her way through the crowded lobby until she was within earshot of the two men. "Ben," she called, as she walked towards them. "I need to talk to you. Hi, Billy," Heather smiled at the young man. "I need to talk to Ben for a minute. Will you please excuse us?"

"Sure, no problem," Billy smiled. "I'll just go see if I can find the guys." He took a clumsy step backward and pointed over his shoulder. "I'll meet you in the groom's room, Ben." He checked his watch. "We've got about twenty minutes."

"Thanks, Billy" Heather smiled.

"Yeah, thanks Billy," Ben added.

When the groom was out of earshot, Heather turned her attention back to Ben. "You haven't told Billy about the conversation we had on the phone last night, have you?"

Ben shook his head. "No. I was a little confused by the whole thing. I didn't want to say anything to him until I'd talked to you."

Heather gave a sigh of relief. "Good."

"Are you here to arrest Sarah?" Ben asked. "On the phone last night, just before we got cut off, it sounded like she was your number one suspect. I still can't believe it," Ben shook his head. "Billy is going to be crushed."

"Slow down, Ben. We aren't here to arrest Sarah, we're here to arrest Jane Phillips."

"What?"

"Come on." Heather took Ben by the arm and led him to a more secluded spot in the lobby. "We have reason to believe that Jane Phillips is responsible for the Brandon Furniture Store fire, and the apartment fire that killed Tom, Scott and Gord."

"Ben looked at her in confusion. "I don't understand, how is there a connection?"

"Well, we know that Brandon's was torched. Investigations at Tom's fire told us that it was arson too."

"What does any of this have to do with Jane?"

"When the boys were inside doing clean- up after the fire,

they found a safe that contained some very damaging evidence. There was a tape of Michael Wells and Jane Phillips doing the horizontal mambo. If something like this ever got out, it could ruin Jane's career!"

"Heather, I still don't understand what one fire has to do with the other."

"Well, the apartment fire that killed Tom, started in the suite of one of Jane's co-workers, Kurt Roper. He's the one who had the videotape. He claims he was planning on giving it back to her. My take on the whole thing is that he was blackmailing her with it."

"So, you think Jane set the fire to get the tape back?"

"I'm not one hundred percent sure. I don't trust this Roper guy. He seems to be somewhat of a slime ball."

Ben gave her a strange look. "You know, come to think of it, I met him at Tom's funeral. He was talking to Katherine and I happened to walk in on the conversation. He mentioned something about the fire being arson. When I asked him where he'd gotten his information, he told me he had buddies on the police force."

"It was arson alright," Heather agreed. "We tested for accelerants and found both gasoline and lighter fluid. After we found the video in Roper's apartment, we got a search warrant for Jane's apartment. There, we found more video tapes." Heather's face turned red with embarrassment. "Jane was in some very interesting positions with some very interesting people. We also found the same brand of lighter fluid that was used on the sofa in this guy's apartment."

Heather took a deep breath. "Dick is on his way to arrest her now. I asked him to wait until tomorrow so he wouldn't screw up Billy and Sarah's wedding, but he wouldn't hear of it."

Ben shook his head in disbelief. "I better go find Rachel and tell her. Jane is in the wedding party. This is sure going to put a real monkey wrench into things."

Chapter Forty Three

SARAH STOOD ALONE IN the bride's room examining her reflection in the full-length mirror. The form fitting, floor length ivory silk gown was perfect. She was perfect. Life was perfect and nothing, or no one, would ever change that.

Since last night, she'd been terrified that her wedding would never take place. She was afraid she would be arrested before she had a chance to walk down the aisle. All day long, she'd been waiting for the police to show up with handcuffs, but they hadn't. Sarah checked her watch. It was 7:50 pm "If the police aren't here by now, they're not coming." She told her reflection with confidence.

"Are you talking to yourself again?" Jane asked as she entered the room in her grand fashion. "How does the dress look? Do you think it's a bit too loose? Maybe I should have had it taken in." She walked to the mirror and gently moved Sarah out of the way.

"I can hear Hark the Herald Angels playing," Rachel announced from the doorway. "Didn't the wedding coordinator mention that was the signal that your guests were in their places?"

A nervous smile lit up Sarah's face. "Yes, she did. So I guess it's time." She took a step forward and stumbled on the hem of her dress. "I knew this was going to happen! I should have gotten it shortened!" She reached down in a flap and pulled the hem of her gown over her knees. "Look, I've ruined it."

"Where's your blue leg band?" Katherine asked.

"What?" Sarah looked down at her legs. "Oh, my God. I

forgot it." She bounced anxiously from foot to foot. "I left it upstairs in my room!"

"We don't have time to go and get it," Rachel told her. "The wedding is about to start."

"Do you have the rest of it?" Katherine asked.

Sarah shook her head. "The rest of what?"

"Something old, something new and something borrowed?" Jane told her.

Sarah reached down the front of her low cut gown until she felt the edge of her white lace bra. The item she was looking for was absent. "I can't believe this. I forgot the white linen handkerchief that belonged to my mother." Sarah raised her arm in the air and stared at her naked wrist. "And I forgot the bracelet Billy gave me for a wedding present too." Tears rolled down her rosy red cheeks. "What am I going to do?"

"Don't you worry your pretty little head," Jane told her. "I've got something that will take care of everything. Something old, new, borrowed and blue." She reached under the collar of her velvet bridesmaid dress and grabbed for the chain that hung around her neck.

"Sarah Baker," the tall dark haired man announced as he burst into the room.

"Yes, I'm Sarah Baker. What can I do for you?" She asked.

He reached inside his coat and pulled out a badge. "I'm Homicide Detective Dick Dickerson with the Seattle Police Department."

When he held his badge in the air, Sarah felt her legs turn to jelly. The color drained from her face. This was it. Her life was over. The police were here to arrest her for killing Michael.

She still wasn't sure if she had actually done it. According to her shrink, the recurring dream was a result of a conversation she'd overheard describing Michael's death. Imagining herself as his killer was brought on by her anger for him.

"I'm looking for Jane Phillips," the detective announced, as he scouted the faces in the room.

Jane pushed her way past Sarah. "I'm, Jane Phillips." She

gave the detective her best smile and offered him her hand as he approached.

When they were standing face to face, Dick pulled a piece of paper from inside his coat and handed it to the tall blonde. "And I, have a warrant for your arrest." He took Jane by the arm, spun her around and slapped a pair of handcuffs on her wrists.

The last thing Sarah heard before she hit the floor were the words: "You have the right to remain silent."

Chapter Forty Four

KATHERINE DABBED A COLD cloth on Sarah's forehead. "Are you feeling better, dear?" She asked when the young girl opened her eyes.

"Yes," Sarah answered in a whisper. "What happened?"

"You fainted, dear," Katherine smiled.

"Where is everyone? The last thing I remember is that detective person.

"Jane has been arrested, Sarah."

"Arrested! Arrested for what?"

"She's been arrested for suspicion of arson. The police took her away. Ben is talking to the wedding guests and Rachel is trying to rustle up some more champagne."

Sarah's bottom lip started to quiver. "My wedding has turned into a nightmare, Katherine. How did this happen?" She held her head in her hands and started to cry.

"There, there dear, it's okay." Katherine put her arm around Sarah's shoulder. "We're not going to let this little incident with Jane ruin the wedding, are we?"

"Everything is good to go," Rachel smiled as she bounced into the bride's room. "You may be getting married later than you had planned, Sarah, but you're still getting married just the same."

"What about the wedding guests," Sarah sniffled. "What did you tell them?"

"You don't have to worry about the wedding guests. The hotel staff has everything under control. They've brought up food and champagne to keep them occupied a little while longer. I thought you may need a few more minutes."

"But they all saw Jane being taken out by the police. What are they going to think?"

"Heather Kennedy asked the detective to remove Jane's handcuffs, which he was nice enough to do, and Ben told the guests who saw her leaving the hotel, that there was some type of a family emergency. So, everything is going to be fine."

"Does Tony know what's going on?" Sarah asked.

"Yes, unfortunately," Rachel frowned. "Ben gave him the rental car. He followed Jane to the Banff police station. Ben said he'd meet him there after the ceremony."

"And Jane? What's going to happen to Jane?" Sarah asked. "I don't understand how all of this happened. I thought I knew Jane. I liked her. How could she be responsible for killing firefighters?"

"I'm sure she isn't," Rachel re-assured Sarah. "I'm sure that this is all just a big mistake. Once Jane gets back to Seattle, and talks to the police, this will all be straightened out."

"I hope you're right."

"I'm sure, I'm right. Besides, you have more important things to think about right now. You have a handsome firefighter waiting to make you his wife."

"She's right," Katherine smiled.

"Okay, I guess I'm ready." Sarah stood up and gave Rachel and Katherine a group hug. "Talking to both of you always makes things better. Have either one of you ever thought about being a shrink?"

There was a soft tap at the door and Katherine went to answer it. "Oh, come in Ben. Is everything okay?"

"All is well in the world," he smiled. He walked to Sarah and took her hands in his. "Everything is ready. Billy is waiting for you. Are you good to go?"

"Yes," she blushed.

"Pete is outside. He's going to walk you down the aisle."

"I guess we're ready then," Rachel smiled. "See, Sarah, I told you that everything would work out."

Sarah took a deep breath. "Let's do it."

"I'll see you girls up front," Ben winked. As he walked past Rachel, he leaned over and whispered in her ear. "I'll see all of you, later."

Her body gave a shiver when the warmth of his tongue found her ear. "I can't wait," she moaned. "Promise me something?"

"What?"

"I don't want to be rude or anything, but as soon as dinner is over, do you think we can retire to our suite." She pressed her firm breasts into his chest. "We'll discuss our wedding, starting with the wedding night!"

"That works for me." He put his arm around her waist, bent towards her and kissed her on the forehead. "You look beautiful, by the way."

"Thank you," Rachel blushed. "You're not too shabby yourself, Captain. The dress uniform is quite becoming." She looked up at him and a seductive grin danced across her face. "Too bad I'm going to have to rip it off of you later."

"We'd better get going before I take you right here on the couch," Ben moaned.

"If you two are finished groping each other," Bruce announced from the doorway, "do you think we can get this show on the road? I have one anxious rookie waiting in a room down the hall."

"Sure thing, Bruce," Ben chuckled. He looked back at Rachel and grinned. "I think I can wait for an hour or so."

Chapter Forty Five

ONE BY ONE, THE members of the wedding party left the bride's room. As they walked through the lobby, hotel guests stopped and smiled at the blushing bride and offered her their congratulations.

When the group reached the small banquet room that would act as a wedding chapel, Ben gave Sarah a fatherly kiss on the cheek. "I've seen a lot of brides in my life, Sarah, but none as beautiful as you."

She threw her arms around him and gave him a big hug. "Oh, thank you, Ben. You are the closest thing I've had to a father in years. You have no idea how much it means to me that you and Rachel did all of this for Billy and me."

"Rachel's the one who put it all together. I just directed traffic."

"Rachel, how can I ever thank you?" Sarah gave her surrogate sister a peck on the cheek.

"You can thank me, by not crying." Rachel lifted Sarah's veil and dabbed at the corner of her eyes with a tissue. "You're going to smudge your make-up. Save the tears until after the wedding, okay?"

"Okay," Sarah grinned.

"Well, I will leave you ladies to do your last minute thing," Ben beamed. "I'm going up front to join the groom."

Rachel called after him as he turned to leave. "Ben, once you're up front, tell the soloist to give us a minute before she starts singing the Lord's Prayer."

"Sure thing."

"Are you ready to go, Katherine?" Bruce asked as he offered her his arm. "I understand that you're filling in for the mother-of-the-bride."

"I sure am," she smiled proudly. Katherine gave Sarah a big hug. "I'll talk to you, when your Mrs. Billy Simpson."

"Oh, God, I'm so nervous," Sarah told Rachel as she watched Bruce and Katherine walk down the aisle.

"There's nothing to be nervous about. Right, Pete?" Rachel gave the lieutenant a broad smile.

"Rachel's right, Sarah. I've got five girls, all married. I'm a trained professional."

Sarah felt her body tense as the organ began to play.

"You ready to go?" Rachel asked.

"Yes."

"Let's do it." Rachel had taken no more than two steps when Sarah grabbed her shoulder.

"Wait, I can't do this."

Rachel spun around to face Sarah. "What do you mean you can't do this?"

"I don't have the stuff I need."

Rachel gave her a confused look. "What stuff? What are you talking about?'

"The wedding stuff! The old and blue and borrowed things that Jane was going to give me."

"Is that all you're concerned about?" Rachel smiled. "You don't have to worry. We can take care of that right now."

Rachel moved Sarah from the doorway. "I was saving these for Ben's and my wedding, but..." She put her hand against the wall for support, and kicked off her right shoe. "Quick, take off your shoe," Rachel ordered as she bent down and scooped her cream colored satin pump off the floor. She shook out the three items that had been resting inside and held them in the palm of her hand. "Hurry, Sarah, give me your shoe."

"Why do you want my shoe?" Sarah asked.

"You want the something old and something new don't you?" Rachel answered.

Sarah shook her head. "Yes, yes I do."

"Then give me your shoe."

Sarah handed Pete her bouquet. "Would you please hold this for me."

"Sure thing," Peter winked.

Sarah followed Rachel's instructions and handed over the footwear. "Here."

"Thanks," Rachel smiled as she took the pump from Sarah's trembling hand. "This will cover most of your bases. Something old, new, and blue."

Sarah's face lit up like a child Christmas morning as she waited in anticipation of the good luck charms that would start her new life off on the right foot.

"These have always brought me luck." Rachel held up the shoe and dropped in three rings: Travis Greenwoods', her Uncle Henry's and the ring she'd been give when she worked for the Chicago Fire Department.

ISBN 1-41201671-1